PRIMAVE

*

Primavera

Grotesqueries

Hayden Thorne

Published by Hayden Thorne, 2023.

Also by Hayden Thorne

A Most Unearthly Rival
The Haunted Inkwell
The House of Creeping Dolls

Grotesqueries
A Castle for Rowena
The Rusted Lily
Primavera

Masks
Masks: The Original Trilogy
Curse of Arachnaman
Mimi Attacks!
Dr. Morbid's Castle of Blood
The Porcelain Carnival

Standalone
Renfred's Masquerade
Rose and Spindle
Gold in the Clouds
Helleville
Icarus in Flight
Arabesque
Banshee
Wollstone
The Glass Minstrel
Henning
The Twilight Gods
The Book of Lost Princes
The Winter Garden and Other Stories

Desmond and Garrick
The Cecilian Blue-Collar Chronicles

Watch for more at https://haydenthorne.com.

Table of Contents

Author's Note

This long novella is an expansion (really, more of a massive overhaul) of a previously published shorter work, which I released in 2015. I've always thought Adam's story needed a more detailed and better developed treatment, hence this longer version. The erotic epilogue was preserved (but shortened) as well as the final scene in the church between Adam and his (other) father.

Chapter 1

I watched the cheap black beads catch and reflect light between my fingers. My rosary was something like my security blanket which I carried around with me but never showed to anyone. Old habits die hard, as they say, and these prayer beads had been mine since my First Communion—a gift from my Irish grandparents. Did they bring me luck? Couldn't really say since life still happened to me, I guess.

I loved the old San Tadeo mission church. I'd always loved how the sunlight streamed through the windows of this old building, bathing the interior in this warm glow that always inspired me to meditate. Not necessarily pray outright as I'd been taught, but just sit there and take in the silence and the quietly praying devotees scattered around me.

It was also the day of the week when Socorro Garza practiced on the old-fashioned pipe organ in the balcony, adding to the atmosphere of the church. Listening to her play my favorite of her practice pieces—also a pretty popular one used in weddings, apparently—would have to be the highlight of my non-praying visits to San Tadeo church.

I asked her once, and she said it was by Bach, and it was called "Jesu, Joy of Man's Desiring". It always calmed me, listening to this specific piece of music. It also sounded the best when played on a gigantic pipe organ that, according to Ms. Garza, was a musical instrument that actually came from Mexico and was over a hundred years old. It was meant to be a replica of the original pipe organ that had been used in the church centuries ago.

Pretty cool, I'd said when she told me, and she grinned, nodded, and gently patted my cheek.

"Yes, it's pretty cool. You love it so much, so maybe you should take lessons?" she said.

"I'm worse than useless when it comes to musical instruments. Besides, shouldn't I be something like a prodigy and start really young to be good at it?"

She snorted. "You love music, right? Okay, then—it's never too late to learn."

I just laughed. Easier said than done, I thought, when it was someone who'd devoted their entire life to music. Ms. Garza said she hung around her local church in Tlaquepaque "forever" as a little girl and befriended the church organist who'd become her instructor. I always thought she never married because, like a nun, she'd entered a holy covenant with the pipe organ—especially one that came from Mexico and was a hundred years old.

That day, though, I was in the restored old mission church because I was just fired from my job at the theater. Too many fuck-ups, I guess, because my head hadn't been on straight for a while now—ever since I turned nineteen. Too many bad nights in bed, waking up from dreams or nightmares I couldn't even remember, and all those really showed in the way I performed at work.

I'd left the candy cart out in the lobby because I completely spaced out—more than once. Naturally, people took advantage of that and swiped a bunch of the stuff on their way in and out of the theater—more than once.

"You're such a fucking retard," Brittany, one of the girls I worked with at the snack counter would say every time while I scrambled to save whatever was left of the candy and take the cart back to the storage room.

"Bitch, you haven't looked in a mirror, have you?" someone else had said the last day I worked with a full crew—I couldn't remember who.

I was already off and running, red-faced and humiliated, my blood pounding in my ears and blocking out nearly every sound. I'd like to think it was Kiki, my best girl buddy at work. She also didn't give a fuck.

On this day, I'd left the candy cart out one too many times, and my boss fired me halfway through my shift. I was just glad it was a weekday, the theater was barely alive with a handful of seniors and mothers with their kids, and Brittany was in school. I was still wearing my stupid uniform, too, but at least I had my hoodie on as well, which made me look a little less like an idiot.

I really should be praying the rosary and meditating and all that given what'd just happened. But I found I couldn't. I'd whipped out my rosary beads and took to just feeling them between my fingers, completely blanking out and letting Ms. Garza's music flow around me and calm me down.

Should I tell my parents about my dreams? They'd probably tell me to pray it all away; otherwise, it'd be therapy. Dad would likely say it was a phase and that I was just adjusting to life after high school. Then he would launch into a passive-aggressive lecture about my life choices at nineteen and the fact that I'd decided to go to a community college and not straight to a four-year university.

Oh, and why the hell would I choose English Lit for a major with a minor in Art History when the money and job security nowadays came from STEM?

Mom would just cry and blame my recent coming out before taking it all back and then telling me it was okay for me to be gay. It was okay as long as I was at peace with being a practicing Catholic and that I wasn't throwing myself into my "lifestyle" with blinders on. I'd realized eventually she believed it was a choice, and I was also going through a phase. That it was best for her to give me space and let me find my way—preferably back to God and eventually blessing her and Dad with a wife and five kids.

Now and then a worshipper would leave or enter the church while I continued to sit on one of the rear pews directly under the balcony where Ms. Garza played the most beautiful music I'd ever heard.

I closed my eyes and just let the rest of the world fall away and fill the void with Bach's music. In the darkness behind my eyelids, I noticed a few other sounds working their way into my head. Subtle sounds, barely audible, and not at all a part of the present world.

Stronger! With more feeling! Like this: dum-dum-DUM-DAH! Presto, son! Presto! Good!

"Wow, that must be some fun stuff in your head."

I gave a start and blinked my eyes open. Ms. Garza stood just outside the narrow iron gate that blocked people from going up the stairs to the balcony. She carried her music books and a set of keys, which she'd already used to lock the gate. I didn't even realize she'd already finished her practice.

"Oh! I was just thinking—meditating, I guess." I shrugged weakly. How long did I space out?

"Sure. Must've been a real hottie to make you lose track of time while 'meditating' inside a holy church."

There was nothing more embarrassing than being teased by a sixty-something Catholic lady who, like Kiki, clearly didn't give a fuck. Ms. Garza was the one who caught on first that I was gay, and she was the first person I came out to. She also just smiled, said a few words in Spanish, and then winked at me. I figured she was cool with me being gay and Catholic since I didn't burn San Tadeo down just by walking through the entrance.

"It wasn't like that!"

"Sure."

She was also pretty fond of saying "Sure" when I fumbled because I was obviously pretty bad at hiding behind almost-lies and even truths. She did admit she liked seeing me blush because my complexion was "vampire-white" according to her, which looked even more undead against my brown-black hair and light gray eyes. I couldn't help my genetics, I used to argue, but that only made me blush even more and draw a triumphant coo from her.

"Well," I said with whatever dignity I could scrape up, "I was listening to your music. I mean it's pretty obvious I like the stuff."

She softened then and sat down beside me. I smelled the familiar lingering smell of medicated pain ointment and baby powder on her—a combination that would likely sicken other people, but its strong connection to Socorro Garza only made it second in comfort levels to my rosary beads. We didn't talk for a few seconds and simply watched the worshippers come and go in reverential silence while the sunlight blessed them.

"You're wearing your uniform," she said under her breath. "What happened?"

I sighed and dropped my gaze back to the rosary beads still tangled with my fingers. "I got fired. Too many fuck-ups. Oh, sorry. Too many mistakes."

"Ah. Another bad night, Adam?"

"Yeah. I don't know how many hours I managed to get, but—last night would have to be the worst so far. I couldn't function at work and—messed up big time. Well, messed up big time for the last time, I guess."

I laughed weakly and shrugged, suddenly feeling the weight of failure and dreading the fallout when I told my parents about what happened. I was sure Dad would just give off that barest hint of justified smugness like he always did whenever I proved him right by making bad choices.

He thought the theater was beneath me, and I should've aimed for something more meaningful and productive even if it had been just a part-time job while I went to school. Mom would take my side, but her heart would likely be breaking all the same because my lifestyle was affecting my chance at success—a punishment from God, very likely.

Ms. Garza nodded, her gaze thoughtful and probing as she watched me until I squirmed.

"I bought a box of Earl Grey tea yesterday," she said at length. "I also made *empanadas de fruta*. Come along. I'd hate to waste all that good shit."

"We're in a church!"

"I know. And God blessed us with the ability to make good shit. Amen."

I laughed quietly, shaking my head, while she stood up and shuffled off to the side aisle while waving me over with a weird mix of impatience and indulgence. I followed her all the same because I might be a loser, but I knew better than to turn down hot tea and homemade Mexican pastries.

As I followed Ms. Garza to her home—just two blocks away from San Tadeo church—my thoughts kept wandering to the strange voice I'd somehow made up in my head back there. What a bizarre thing to pull out of thin air, especially when I didn't even know what the context was. It sounded like a teacher, anyway, but I'd no idea what this teacher would be going on about with all that stuff about feeling and strength and something about presto. I guess I must have been a hell of a lot more messed up in the head from so many bad nights than I'd first thought.

Chapter 2

1 January, 17—Mamma breathed her last today. She could barely speak when I sat at her bedside, but she had strength enough to open her eyes and look at me, smiling.

"You take care of your poor father," she said in a half-whisper, and I held her hand in both of mine. She was too thin and too cold. It took me all the strength I had not to break down in front of her now that I'm the only pair of shoulders Papà could lean on.

She saw right through me in spite of everything. She'd always said I was too open and guileless for my own good. Mamma shook her head and added, "It's perfectly all right to cry, my love. Even angels weep in heaven, don't you know?"

I burst into tears then and shook my head. I didn't want to. Once I started, I wouldn't be able to stop, and I wanted my final moments with my mother to be coherent. Who says goodbye to a parent with nonsensical stutters? I was determined not to be that person, but I failed myself and Mamma.

"Work hard on your music," she said despite my blubbering. Her voice took on a hint of strength then as though she knew she was only seconds away from death. "You were born with a rare gift. It's a terrible sin to ignore or trivialize it, Paolo. And it's even worse if it's abused for selfish purposes. Do you hear me?"

I could only nod.

I write what I can remember of our final conversation, but grief's still too heavy for me to keep a clear enough head for this. Mamma went on about my talent in music, how my gifts showed unnaturally early. How I took to a distant cousin's harpsichord at five, climbing the instrument and pounding my fists up and down the keyboard before testing it with restlessly moving fingers. How our next visit the year after showed me playing nursery songs from memory and somehow managing to find the right key for each note.

Mamma ordered me to work doubly hard once she's gone because Papà would need all the financial help he could get. She'd watch over us both in heaven, she said. She'd make sure neither of us would put a foot wrong. She'd guide me as sure as the sun rises and sets each day. I bent down to kiss her sunken cheek, and she kissed mine back. Her last words were "Sing freely, boldly, and lovingly—my beautiful nightingale!"

The house is silent, and I still haven't dressed for bed. I must look like an absolute disaster, weeping on and off all day. I'd seen to Papà some hours ago, and he now sleeps alone for the first time in over twenty years though he required a bit of help from the doctor's sleeping tonic. He spent a good deal of time in church, praying to the Virgin in the side chapel. I was only able to pray for a few minutes before grief and exhaustion broke me once again, but Papà gently urged me to see to my needs while he carried on with his task.

"Give me time, Paolo. I need more time."

It's too bad time is never guaranteed to anyone, but knowing my father, he'll move heaven and earth to defy that fact. I learned early on to allow him his impossible dreams, which he spins endlessly in that mind of his when it comes to me and Mamma. But he only has me now to defy time for, and I hope I'm deserving of his dreams, fantastical or no.

*

7 March, 17—Signora Salvaggio and her family are moving to Seville. The poor lady was quite distraught over the mere act of breaking the bad news to me that she actually forgot herself completely and cried. I reassured her it was all right (it wasn't, really) and that opportunities for her husband ought to be pursued for the sake of her children. I'm going to miss teaching Beppe and Cecilio, but the twins will find another music teacher at their new home. I extracted a promise from poor Signora Salvaggio regarding the boys' music education though she complained she'd likely fail to find another prodigy.

Prodigy, hardly! I might be lucky enough to be gifted in music, but a prodigy? Surely I'd be performing before kings and queens by now, not to mention composing and publishing operas or something if that were so! Isn't that how these things go, anyway?

I've been told, though, that such luck is rare for someone in my shoes, and money talks. As things stand, I'm rather poor and can only go so far even with my talent, but I know better than to overreach. At least Papà continues to remind me to be humble despite my constant itching for something bigger and—dare I say it—better.

Poor Papà. I broke the news to him over dinner, when he was dreadfully tired from another long day working on what he calls a "vanity fresco" for a gentleman with more money than sense. At least the pay's good, but new work's awfully difficult to come by once the current job's done.

He took the news well enough, I think, but I saw the light in his eyes dimming. We live practically hand-to-mouth with Mamma no longer adding to the pot with her sewing. This is a great blow, and I hope to find something new quickly. At least the Salvaggio family won't be leaving till the end of the month, and I'm still employed till then. That ought to give me some time to look around.

*

19 March, 17—Signorina Amatore's showing progress. Slowly but surely, her confidence grows now that she's no longer so self-conscious about her "tentacle fingers" as she often calls them because they're long and thin. The child's only ten, but she'll surely bloom in music and may even be a proper wife and hostess and entertain friends and guests with impeccable playing someday. It's too bad her father never thought to have her taught sooner despite her keen interest in music.

The family even owns a harpsichord my pupil admits to sneaking a bit of time on whenever her father was out on business before I was hired. The servants have learned to turn a blind eye to the lonely little thing since her mother—like mine—has "been reclaimed by the angels"—and, like me, she's the only child. Signor Amatore never remarried and has been far too busy making money to think about finding another wife. Young Maddalena is taught by a lady who doesn't stay with the family, strangely enough, though I understand she used to.

"She lived with us for a year," Maddalena said during a break in lessons, "but she suddenly decided to pack up and leave while keeping her position as my governess. Though—does that make her my governess still since she's no longer here all day, every day?"

"I think so. You might be confusing her for a nurse, which you really don't need anymore," I replied. "As long as the lady still teaches you, she's a governess."

The child still requires a female companion, however, and a servant is always in the room with us when I come for our lessons. We do talk openly before the servant, but I noticed Maddalena always took to low whispers when she talked about her governess. I suspect she didn't want the servant to hear and perhaps report back to the father. I wonder now if there's something more to the story, but my pupil's at that age where theatrics are quite common, and I'm likely just overblowing things.

Papà's fresco project's nearing its conclusion, and he did say he'd like to take a bit of a break before accepting another commission. He's been working non-stop since Mamma died, and I know he did so to distract himself from the loss. I hope this is a sign he's doing better and is willing to take care of himself with some much-deserved rest.

*

22 March, 17—Beppe and Cecilio were unmanageable today! The boys aren't happy about the move to Seville, and I couldn't get them both to settle down. I had to threaten calling their mother into the room, but that didn't seem to deter them. In fact, things only got worse.

A botched day still meant I get paid for it, but I can't sleep with the thought that I got paid for nothing. Papà always told me to keep trying when something like this happens. So I threatened, I begged, I cajoled, and if I had the means for it, I'd have bribed the children, but nothing worked.

A good deal of sulking and half-hearted playing rewarded my pains, and I'd have torn my hair out had Cecilio not attached himself to me in a tight and awkward embrace when I prepared to leave.

"Can you not come with us?" he asked before bursting into tears. At that point a red-faced and flustered nurse had to pry him off me and carry him away. I thought the walls of the house would come down around me with Cecilio's piercing shrieks while Beppe, red-eyed, shadowed them like a silent ghost. Signora Salvaggio was very apologetic and even offered an increase in my pay for the rest of the month. I had to decline in the end since my last lesson with the boys was in a week.

I ended my day with a terrible headache. I'm also heartbroken over the loss of my little pupils. I'll miss them, to be sure, and I sincerely hope they continue their lessons with another. Surely there's someone in Seville who's just as desperate as I am in finding work as a private music teacher.

*

25 March, 17—Signor Amatore surprised me and Maddalena with a visit during the last hour of today's lessons. No one knew he was planning to return home early, but the gentleman assured me he'd meant it to be a special surprise for his daughter.

"I know I haven't been there for her as often as I should have," he confessed when we took a break before the last half hour. Maddalena had to withdraw for a few minutes in the company of a servant, and I was left alone with her father. "Thank you, signore, for helping my daughter. Truly, I've never seen her so happy and so proud of herself."

A shadow crossed his features then, and he spoke at length about his late wife. I thought it was rather odd, but while he said all the right words one expects from a grieving widower, I saw no real passion in his face. No physical expression of grief and love that felt convincing.

Then again, I also wondered if I was being unfair because given my own loss, I'm now judging how others deal with theirs. It isn't right, is it? I, of all people, should know better and be more charitable toward my employer. Next time I'll do better and be more sympathetic. He did promise to be there for the entire lesson now that he's seen what I can do, he said. I'm very pleased!

Chapter 3

The fallout never happened, to my surprise, but I did take full advantage of the bag of *empanadas de fruta* that Ms. Garza gave me.

"Trust me, they'll help you. Serve them while working the bad news into the conversation. Your parents will never know what hit them," she'd said, shoving the bag into my hands. She'd also tossed them all into a paper grocery bag and filled it halfway, so one could only imagine how loaded I was with delicious bribes.

And she was right. A quick warm-up in the microwave, and I was golden.

"The college should have some part-time positions you can look into," Dad said, practically cooing over the warm pastries. We still had a couple of hours till dinner, and the pastries would surely ruin our appetites, but nobody cared because we were all big fans of Ms. Garza's baking. "Mike—remember Mike, honey?—his daughter's a lab assistant at her community college. The Chemistry Department, I think, hired her."

"It doesn't have to be something related to your major if your department isn't hiring at the moment," Mom added with a pleased nod. "Talk to someone—even your adviser if he's available—and be really proactive about this. We want to see you succeed."

I didn't look at Dad at that moment as I'd hate to see whatever look he might have had at the mention of success. If there was something there, it was obviously tempered by Ms. Garza's pastry distraction. By the end of our group gluttony hour, we couldn't think of dinner without gagging, but we at least made sure to leave ourselves half of what I'd brought home. For tomorrow's lunch packs—or Mom and Dad's. I was going to be stuck at home, sorting through job postings online after school if things didn't pan out there.

I didn't say a word about my disturbed nights. Not a word about the dreams and nightmares that'd been the cause of my problems in the day. I didn't want to think about where *that* conversation would lead. It was one thing to admit I messed up in a big way at work that led me to being fired. It was another completely to tell my parents the reason behind my perpetual brain fog, which, I'm sure, wasn't common among people my age.

I couldn't even function in school and had a really tough time concentrating. In a desperate move, I started physically writing the lectures and was pretty much the only student who didn't use a laptop for my notes. I figured writing things down the old-fashioned way with a pen and paper (and in cursive) would force my brain to clear itself, and it worked. To a point, it did.

When I got home from school, I'd take a shower and then fall into bed for a long nap while my parents were still at work. No dreams and nightmares bothered me then, and I was able to rewrite and organize my lecture notes—also in longhand.

That night I did go over several job listings online, and my school's website didn't offer anything that interested me.

By the end of the day, I was able to submit my updated resume to a bunch of entry-level positions in a wide variety of industries. The theater job had been my first—not a good look for me—but I figured as someone who was only just starting out, I'd be cut a little more slack compared to someone who'd been working much longer. Maybe the "teen" in "nineteen" would give me a bit of an edge in some ways.

* * * *

Half of the places I applied to didn't respond to my application, and half practically wanted me to start right *now*. But only one place really interested me, and that was a small production warehouse for picture frames and art. I figured my minor in Art History would work to my advantage, and maybe I'd be exposed to all kinds of art that would expand my interests further and help me in school.

The interview happened the next day, and I was afraid I went through the whole thing looking really stupid with my eyes bugging out and my jaw hitting the ground as the manager gave me a tour of the place.

"We need to fill a couple of positions in the ready-made area," he said as he led me through a pretty loud space with different saws and joiners going on at the same time.

He pointed out the racks of empty frames ready to be worked on as well as the pneumatic guns, pallets of precut glass, and boxes of hardware, describing the actual job and what was expected from me if I were hired.

The ready-made half of the facility had a row of pretty large tables where empty frames were assembled with glass, slip sheets, cardboard, and pre-packaged hardware before being shrink-wrapped, bundled, and then sent out to different stores who placed orders with the company. The other half of the place was for framing art, and that was for people with pretty specific experiences.

As we passed the worktables in that half of the warehouse, my gaze fell on one of the prints being worked on by a middle-aged man, and I almost tripped.

It was a print of a group of shepherds crowding around a large rectangular stone with something written on it. There were trees around them, and the stone looked like it didn't belong in that scene and yet it did. A woman who also looked different from the shepherds hovered beside them, looking rather creepy with her calm presence while the shepherds seemed nervous and even slightly freaked out.

I didn't know what that print was, but the image really struck me because—somehow—I'd seen it before. The feeling was so strong, the conviction behind it nearly blindsiding me, and I had to stop by that workstation, staring like an idiot at the print. The manager had to stop talking and double back to my side, looking a little confused now.

"See anything interesting?" he asked blandly.

I knew I was risking messing up my interview, but I couldn't help myself. Before I could say anything, though, the man who was working on it grinned at me.

"You like art?" he asked.

"I do. I'm studying Art History—well, as a minor, I mean," I stammered. I couldn't take my eyes off that print because my brain was furiously scrambling after that odd feeling of familiarity.

"I like that print, too. It's Nicholas Poussin. You'll be running across him in your classes."

"What's this one called?" I asked.

"*The Arcadian Shepherds*. It's also called *Et in Arcadia Ego*. What do you think?"

I blinked and finally glanced up to meet his gaze. Kindness and a cheerful personality beamed at me from behind thick glasses, and he softened his grin to a smile that felt very fatherly. I drew a shaky little breath at that but managed to keep my head together that time.

"I really like it. I've never seen anything like that before even though—even though it feels as if I have."

"Ah. Well, it's pretty famous—at least to us art geeks." He winked and laughed. "If you've been online looking through art sites, you likely came across this. You just don't remember."

I nodded, still slightly overwhelmed by the weird and unexpected mental blow, but I had to take his word for it. I did spend a lot of time online, looking at art and so on—both classic stuff like this one and more modern art by digital artists.

Why I didn't major in art, no one but I knew. I simply didn't have the talent for it, but I loved it and wanted nothing more than to surround myself with amazing images when I finally got my own place. My home at the moment was pretty spare with only a few family photos gracing our walls, and those were all inherited from my grandparents.

"So, um, do you work on a bunch of stuff like this one?" I asked.

"All kinds. Classic art like this, more modern stuff like Warhol, and even terrific stuff from younger artists no one knows, sadly."

I had to pull myself away reluctantly when the manager reminded me of our interview, and we walked past a few more workstations and artwork in varying stages of completion. I recognized Michelangelo and da Vinci. There was another print of a boy with long, luxurious, wavy hair dressed up as a shepherd (I had to ask the employee for details), and I was told the print was of a painting by Sir Peter Lely—a name I didn't recognize. However, there it was again, that strong and creepy feeling of having seen that image before. Maybe something very, very similar if not the exact one.

For this one, I knew for sure I'd never come across that image online. It seemed too obscure for a quick online search to cough up unless I was looking for something or someone very specific.

By the time we returned to the manager's office, I was so disoriented from the noise, the crazy equipment, and the art that I could barely keep track of the rest of the interview. The manager, bless him, didn't seem to care and even appeared amused by my bizarre reactions to art that they probably see every day. A rundown on different company policies was discussed, and by the end of my interview, I was the newest employee of the warehouse, and the manager—Curtis Sheedy—was going over my preferred schedule with obvious relief.

He was also middle-aged and had "art" screaming from top to bottom. Short, scruffy gray hair, round glasses, a moustache and beard, and he even wore a dress shirt with a vest and corduroy pants. His small office was crammed with stuff he'd bought in his travels to Europe, particularly France, which was his favorite holiday spot.

I felt comfortable around him and especially his office, that strange feeling of familiarity again buzzing but a lot more faintly. I had to look around and take in as many of the odds and ends he'd collected, wondering what it was exactly that had triggered this reaction in me this time around, but I saw nothing that stood out.

Maybe it was just being surrounded by things coming from a specific place that made me fall into this dream-like head space, but it was certainly nowhere near the sudden derailment I experienced out there in the main warehouse. That had been unsettling and almost terrifying, and I actually felt so shaken up by art prints. It was a pretty surreal thing to consider, but it happened, and it still hung around me when I got home. I was sure I went about the rest of my day in a bit of a haze but was clear-headed enough to break the good news to Mom and Dad when they came home from work.

"Well, it's about art, so I suppose that's good," Dad said with bland approval while Mom predictably fretted over the dangerous machines and equipment I'd be exposed to.

I knew, though, that I was going to thrive there.

Chapter 4

30 March, 17—I continue to grieve over the loss of my two twins, but given the success of yesterday's final lessons, I'm confident in their ability to find a new teacher where they're headed. Today has been spent seeing three more families for possible employment, and I succeeded in appealing to one. Unfortunately the other two were awfully demanding and finicky, appearing somewhat dismayed at seeing me so young at nineteen years. Apparently a "true" teacher of music ought to be a gentleman of thirty years or so, and nothing would sway their opinions. I even presented them with recommendations from Signora Salvaggio and Signor Amatore.

I suppose I understand. My music teacher was over sixty when he saw something good in me and took me on. Anyway, the third interview was a success.

At least—like my two past and present employers—Signor Cloutier, recently transplanted from France—is very generous in his compensation, and I'm quite pleased that he's very much a kindly old gentleman who doesn't hold back in lavishing his orphaned grandchildren all the good things the rest of us can only imagine for ourselves.

I wondered at first if their move to Italy was a temporary thing, but Signor Cloutier shook his head.

"I need the splendid warmth of your region, young man. My poor bones are brittle, and the winters in France are proving too much for me now. As for my grandsons, they're old enough to appreciate the change. Indeed, they were much more impatient to move than I was," he replied with a merry twinkle in his fading eyes.

I'll be teaching only one of the two—Jori, who's eleven and who's also quite obsessed with music after watching a private concert in Paris with his parents. The older brother is a half-brother from their father's earlier marriage, the unfortunate lady having succumbed to a wasting illness when Gilles was five.

The most astonishing fact about these two is that there's a fourteen-year gap in their ages, their father having avoided marrying again, convinced he'd never find another woman like his first wife. So Gilles is currently twenty-five.

Signor Cloutier introduced them to me with Jori lingering as I needed to spend a bit of time with my new pupil before our first lesson would commence.

Both are serious young men for their age though I did expect a certain gravity in Gilles given his age. Now he's got a head for business, apparently, and he's intent upon learning more about his new home in hopes of bringing the family business to this region. Marquetry is where their family had enjoyed much success, and it would almost be like bringing such a magnificent art home. He expects to be traveling a great deal all over Italy and back to France for this venture.

Young Jori is even a great deal more solemn and thoughtful than his brother, and I suspect he's got his mind set on priesthood someday. He's a quiet young man but clearly pays very close attention to everything happening around him. I daresay he'll prove to be a promising pupil soon enough.

So all in all the day wasn't a waste though I'd hoped to boast at least two new employers. For the time being, I'll make sure Mamma's strictness and economy are followed to the letter. God knows Papà and I can't afford trivial expenses until I'm hired by one more family.

*

4 April 17—Signor Amatore has decided to increase the number of lessons little Maddalena will have with me. Her confidence continues to grow at a very pleasing rate, and it doesn't take me much to chip away at yet another barrier she's erected around herself out of a misplaced dislike of her appearance. I expect her to bloom into a tall and thin woman with all the qualities of an otherworldly creature—a young goddess of music, I suppose, if I were to be so romantic about her future.

Her father recently learned the truth from the servants regarding her stolen moments on the harpsichord and has coaxed her into a casual performance of her favorite pieces.

"I never knew I had a naturally talented musician right under my nose," he'd said following Maddalena's lesson, and she'd bounded off with a servant, leaving Signor Amatore and I alone in the music-room. "Perhaps even a prodigy. But it's too late to help her develop as a prodigy would, isn't it? She never had lessons at a younger age—never enjoyed the benefit of having you for her teacher."

There was a mournful quality to the gentleman's tone, which was unexpected as I've grown used to a much more subdued and emotionless presence from him. Now that he's spending more time at home and not traveling for business, he's seen his daughter's progress as well as deep passion for music. His conscience must have been hammered badly, and it was gratifying seeing him change his opinion and admit his errors in the way he raised his daughter.

And so now my new schedule is a daily lesson but with the hours changed to the afternoon. Maddalena's governess is going to come in the morning—a reversal of her previous schedule as well as requested by the lady, I was told. I suspect she (like me) is seeing her days quite broken up between more than one pupil. I still don't know why she'd decided to abandon the idea of living with her student, which I thought was more conducive to better pay and a better living situation with all the benefits of housing and good meals.

Perhaps she's like me who simply can't afford to be teaching just one person. Really, I should stop all this speculating as it only makes me look like a dull old gossip.

*

7 April, 17—Papà's "vanity fresco" commission has come to an end, and he's both exultant and dreadfully exhausted. He desperately needs a break for a while, and with my newest string of luck in music-teaching, we can afford his momentary retreat from work. Papà's lost himself too much in his after Mamma died—more than usual, anyway, since he's always been a hard worker and counts himself lucky to be doing exactly the thing he loves most for money.

The gentleman who's now soaring in triumph over his villa's return to the "old Roman ways" was so happy with the results that he's not only paid Papà what he still owed, but added a generous amount to it in gratitude. I suppose he might be vain as Papà said, but at least he was honorable enough to recognize and reward talent and hard work. Papà's work at that villa took him several weeks altogether (I can't even remember exactly when he began at this point) that he's now walking about with sore muscles and joints, and that extra money will help us with Papà's medical expenses. I daresay rest will only take him so far.

"I'm afraid I'm not as young as I used to be, Paolo," he said over dinner. "I was able to recover quickly enough when I was your age, but—God help me, I think I need to lie down for a good month."

We enjoyed a good laugh at his expense, but he was quite sporting about it and has always been wryly humorous about the monstrous changes a body undergoes as it ages. It also helped blessing him with the good news about my new schedule, which will begin tomorrow.

With Signor Cloutier, I'm expected to teach Jori every day as well. Since our lessons won't begin formally till tomorrow, I had the luxury of visiting the gentleman one more time after being summoned there. He and Jori had a good talk about the boy's expectations and desires, and Jori hopes to throw himself fully into music in addition to his regular education. A good deal of planning followed, and Signor Cloutier agreed to a morning schedule for Jori given my prior commitment to Maddalena in the afternoon. He'll be having his regular lessons with his tutor after lunch in a reversal of Maddalena's calendar, which isn't a problem on the whole.

What of school for the boy? That might come down the road—if at all, I was told. Jori had been to school in France, but apparently things didn't go too well for him, and he was instantly withdrawn and had benefited more from one-to-one work with private tutors instead. As always, I didn't pursue that point since it's not for me to ask. Jori will have to tell me himself if he ever feels inclined to share.

*

10 April, 17—I had a peculiar meeting with Maddalena's governess at the market this morning. Signora Tessaro crossed paths with me quite laden with fresh vegetables for this weekend's meals, and we exchanged a few surprised pleasantries.

I didn't recognize her as we've never met before, and I've only known about her from Maddalena's furtive accounts of the lady's sudden change in living situations. However, apparently *she* recognized *me* because she'd seen me a few times leaving the residence while she hovered nearby, waiting her turn to teach our pupil. That had been when I used to tutor my little signorina in the morning, and Signora Tessaro came almost immediately after me.

That point baffled me since being a governess who's been teaching Maddalena for over a year, she should have felt comfortable enough to enter the premises and wait out the time in the sitting-room or something. Strangely enough, she refused to enter until it was precisely her time to be there.

Well, I thought, perhaps she's a good deal more finicky than I'd first thought, which I suppose is a good quality to have in a governess who held her pupil's future in her hands. However, hanging about aimlessly while waiting out the time surely exposes her to all manner of danger.

"Don't be silly!" she said with a bubbly laugh. "I go to the coffeehouse a block away and stay safe within doors. I've gotten quite familiar with the traffic there, you know. It's also a place frequented by a company of local artists, so some unorthodox behavior isn't cause for concern. I feel a great deal safer in *their* company even if I know none of them—much safer than the company of gentlemen of good standing in society's eyes."

I suppose she had a point, I thought, but before I could consider it further, she carried on heedlessly, and we were soon extolling our pupil's virtues to the heavens since we now share the opinion that Maddalena Amatore is a budding genius whose gifts were nearly nipped in the bud by her father's disinterest.

"I understand Signor Amatore now spends his days at his home," she said, and I nodded. She sounded more thoughtful and serious when she spoke then, a crease forming between her brows and making her look more hardened and dour at twenty-five. "Has he been spending a good deal of time in the music room during your lessons?"

From start to finish, I replied, which only deepened the crease and earned me a distracted little nod. I was left blinking for a few seconds before she appeared to rouse herself from her thoughts, and she smiled at me.

"Well—he's just deeply interested in Maddalena's progress. As long as he does nothing more than watch her, all's well." Of course, I thought—what father would do less for his child?

Chapter 5

I walked with dragging steps toward a dimly lit side chapel, and for some reason, the closer I got, the more frightened I felt. I'd had dreams—nightmares—years ago where the more I ran away from something, the slower I got. And the more I felt as though my legs were turning into cement or that I was trying to run through extra thick sludge until whatever it was I was running from caught up with me.

In this instance, I walking *toward* something I didn't want to go to, but the same increasing resistance was there. Not only that—movement *and* an emotional response were forefront.

The side chapel itself was a really old one, and it was barely lit with faint light streaming through three narrow, dusty stained glass windows. I was inside a larger church, whose interior was deeply shadowed though I knew my way around it in spite of the lack of illumination. Not that it mattered, really, since it felt as though whatever was shaping my dream were determined to push me toward the side chapel and nowhere else.

There wasn't anything in the side chapel but what I figured was a statue of the Virgin standing on a low platform of sorts set into a shallow alcove. There were a few votive candles lit up in their containers, which were also displayed on a simple wrought iron candle stand placed against a wall between two of the windows.

The atmosphere in the side chapel could be felt from where I was, and it was nearly crippling.

Grief and mourning—twisted and woven into each other like a heavy, suffocating blanket of sorrow that slowly oozed out as though an old dam just cracked a little, and a gradual flow of water was pushing through it. No doubt it would turn into a major gusher if it weren't stopped.

That overwhelming feeling added to my terror as I closed the distance, and my legs began to shake, my knees locking up. My heart suddenly twisted in my chest as I stared, bug-eyed, at the empty side chapel. I didn't want to go inside; that was the overriding gut feeling that had me in its grip. My heart raced, my blood pumped wildly in my ears, and an awful chill descended on me, making my skin break out in goosebumps.

"No. No, no, no, no, no..."

I mumbled that over and over again into the death-like silence of the church and the side chapel. Then my knees completely gave way, and I crumpled to the stone floor, refusing to move another inch closer. I didn't know how long I stayed there, utterly frozen and locked up, staring in mounting horror at what was really nothing more than a moody, empty space of worship.

But there *was* something wrong with it. I knew it deep, deep down, and once that conviction and accompanying feeling were roused, there was no holding them back. I stayed there, on my hands and knees, unable to move save for the painfully slow way I forced myself into a frightened ball on the floor.

"No, no, no—I won't go there—never..."

Nothing came out of the side chapel. Everything stayed quiet and still, but the feeling of immeasurable and toxic grief and helpless despair flowed out in a steady and brutal stream. It moved around me, over me, and through me, spearing me in place with this horrifying conviction that a disaster had happened in that quiet, unobtrusive space. A private space of worship.

"No, no, no, no..."

No! No, stop! I won't—let me go!

* * * *

I jackknifed up in bed, flailing and getting myself tangled up in my bedclothes. I might have cried out as I was startled awake, but the silence and stillness of the house once my brain cleared itself told me no one had heard. My parents' bedroom was two rooms away, anyway, so I was lucky in that.

My heart stuttered, and my breaths were ragged, and my chest felt so, so tight and painful. I thought at first I was having some kind of heart attack, but the longer I waited, the more I was convinced it was nothing more than an extreme reaction to a weird dream.

I normally didn't remember dreams the moment I woke up, but every now and then, they'd linger in my head a little, and I'd cling to fading images upon waking. Even less than a few would actually stay with me throughout the day, and I figured it had everything to do with how I processed those dreams and how much I mentally held on to them once I was up and about.

For those rare "remnants", as I usually called them, they eventually disappeared from memory over time though maybe a handful of childhood nightmares—recurring ones, especially—could still be recalled with pretty disturbing clarity.

I didn't know what dreams meant given so many theories about their purpose and possible messages. Recurring ones must mean *something,* especially if they happened to a little kid for a good part of his childhood. Or was it a function of a normally developing brain? I didn't know.

At any rate, I was sitting up in bed, waiting for residual terror to flutter off into the night, but the shadows left by that awful feeling pervading my dream stuck around, and I had to rub my arms and discovered they were completely covered in goosebumps. I shuddered and looked around me, anchoring myself with familiar details of my bedroom.

This dream seemed different from those that had disturbed my nights and made me lose my theater job. This one was far more powerful and was a massive punch in the gut, so much so I could actually remember everything I saw and experienced. Those dreams in the past were likely a lot less impactful but definitely potent enough to mess up my nights and leave me exhausted and foggy-headed in the day.

It took me a moment with several deep, calming breaths before peace was restored, and I nervously chided myself for being such a drama queen over a dream. Did it count as a nightmare? Nothing happened in the dream, but the sadness that seemed to ooze out of every inch of stone, paint, and cement in that old side chapel made me rethink my definition of a nightmare.

Sighing, I threw off the blankets and stood up. I kept a small spiral-bound notebook in my dresser, and I thought maybe I should start a dream diary. I'd heard about those, and I'd actually met a couple of people my age who sincerely believed in their benefits and kept up with their habits. Maybe I should write down whatever I *could* remember...

In case worse comes to worst, and I'd be forced to see a therapist, I suppose. At least I'd have something to show them if that were to happen, but I really hoped it wouldn't come to that.

Now that sleep had mostly fled, I had no choice but to sit down and write, taking care to keep my desk lamp set to a low light as I didn't really want to be awake to the point where I wouldn't be able to go back to sleep after. I wrote everything I could remember until I completely exhausted my ability to recall. At least I didn't have to go to school that day, but my first day of work would be an absolute bitch.

At least I proved myself right that time—with the dimmed light, I mean. I might have been clear-headed enough to write my dream down, but eventually all that went away, and I was practically dragging myself back into bed, where I collapsed and succumbed to sleep almost instantly.

My first day on the new job was partly spent filling out all kinds of paperwork, and I was absolutely thrilled to secure a thirty-two-hour schedule, which was the maximum I should have if I wanted to maintain my GPA in school. After that I was shown around again, this time to be introduced to everyone currently working.

And my gaydar obviously worked because I picked out a pretty healthy percentage of the staff as queer, which made a bit of sense since—at least from what I'd observed online at different sites catering to all things artistic, a significant number of people from the queer community gravitated toward the Creative Arts.

Granted, that might not really mean much since my online world had been fairly limited to places that I wanted to enjoy and feel safe in. Being gutsy and bold wasn't in my DNA, and I wasn't one to explore much.

Curtis assigned me to a specific workstation and instructed me on how the company preferred us to approach that day's work log, and the workstation I was given was closest to rolling racks of relatively large frames. Before long I was busy pulling empty frames, setting them face-down on my table, and wandering off to get glass from the necessary pallet.

The noise of the saws and joiners coming from the other end of the warehouse eventually turned into white noise, but Curtis did say I could listen to my own music to block out the sounds if I wanted. I set up my phone to my favorite playlist and plugged in my earbuds. I could get used to this, I thought, happiness finally washing over me as familiar music pushed away the less palatable sounds of industrial equipment, and I was soon in a zone of sorts, finding my rhythm in time with the music: frame, glass, slip sheet, backing, and hardware, all secured together with a flex-tab gun.

It must have been about two hours into my shift and right after my first ten-minute break when I saw him.

Tall, dark-featured—possibly Latino or Spanish—with narrow, sparkling eyes that turned up slightly at the temples, a strong but short nose and full lips—he was beautiful. Pretty, since his features would be considered soft compared to commonly idealized masculine beauty. But he was gorgeous, I thought, and I kept stealing glances at him and was totally thrilled when I saw he worked at the station directly in front of me.

He was also friendly and polite for someone my age (I learned later that he was also nineteen), and he was the one who approached me first and stuck out a hand for me to shake.

"Hi," he said in a well-modulated voice, his smile managing the impossible and making his eyes sparkle even more. It felt like staring at a fairy prince or something, and I must've looked absolutely stupid taking his hand while gaping helplessly at him. "I'm Christian."

"Adam," I replied, still looking more like a goldfish than a high functioning human. "Nice to meet you."

"I was told you're new, and Curtis asked me to help you out if you have questions or anything."

I nodded, swallowing. "Okay, cool. Thank you. And nice meeting you, too, Christian."

I'd have talked to him some more, but he was called away.

Chapter 6

15 April, 17—Maddalena was all a-flutter today, barely able to keep her seat and concentrate on our lessons. Her father was away, but she was dreadfully thrilled over his decision to spend half of his time at home and not elsewhere, doing what he does for business. From what I understand, he really didn't have to be away in the city since business was doing exceedingly well, and he can easily delegate tasks to a few capable employees if he wished and spend more time at home with his daughter.

I'm not one to gossip, but Maddalena's a lonely girl who craves attention from her surviving parent. No amount of fussing and spoiling from servants and the governess will ever take the place of a father's affection. That means she's simply ecstatic beyond words when Signor Amatore announced his decision a few days ago.

"He'll still be traveling when he has to, you know," she said, turning around and facing the wrong direction on the bench. Her feet swung, her hands flapped and waved, and her backside kept bouncing on the cushion. "But he'll be doing all the writing work here. Well, unless he's needed in the city, I suppose. Isn't that exciting, though? Papà's going to be here when we have our lessons!"

It was a real pleasure seeing the girl so happy and bright, to be sure, but I wasn't being paid to listen to her chatter on and on about how lovely things are now compared to before. In my head I had to reconfigure my plans for the week, moving some lessons and possibly shortening others to make up for the wasted time today.

At the same time, however, I was also dependent upon the Amatore family's largesse, and I couldn't be an ogre toward my poor student and risk being sacked.

Maddalena eventually calmed down though she still wasn't fully engaged as she went through her scales. Indeed, majority of what we ended up doing today was just that, leaving us with not much time for the actual pieces meant for today's lessons.

I've never been one to scold a pupil or—just like how *I* was taught—reluctantly strike a pupil's hands with a flat stick when I misbehaved (and which I did far too much, testing poor, kindly Signor Belluomo's patience), but I did talk more sternly with Maddalena until she realized she wasn't going to get her hoped-for response from me.

Perhaps with her father's new schedule, she'll conduct herself appropriately.

*

17 April, 17—Young Jori astonishes me day after day. He truly picks things up a great deal more quickly, and he's never shown an ounce of resentment or impatience when I tell him it isn't time for the next lesson. It's one thing to learn something at an astonishingly fast rate, but it's entirely another to prove the lesson's fully mastered. Jori, bless him, is quiet and introspective as a pupil, and he really does consider everything I tell him, taking whatever time he needs to ponder my instructions or explanations before saying something in turn.

It's almost as though he were born with an old scholar's soul, and it doesn't surprise me at all that he's quite mad over books and the written word. I do believe I'm in the presence of yet another prodigy, but as with Maddalena, poor Jori's talent hadn't been nurtured quickly enough at a much younger age, and now's all about playing catch-up.

That said, while both children will someday play the most exquisite music with the greatest skill, neither will be wooed by Europe's courts. Perhaps one might end up in my shoes, teaching private lessons to wealthy families—although that's usually something only poorer people are forced to do, I suppose.

I did talk about my history when I was being interviewed for the post, and Signor Cloutier was quite dismayed at hearing about the barriers that had kept me from going down the path that other musical greats had taken. It was—had always been—about money. My parents were too poor to afford early lessons for me once my talent was discovered, and they weren't educated enough to understand the scope of success that would have been possible for someone like me.

Whatever natural and unique talent I was born with has been diverted as a result, and I now earn money through less glittering methods. But would I have been happy traveling all over Europe, performing before nobility and aristocracy or even be hired to be a court composer? I honestly can't wrap my head around that idea. I find it too overwhelming and perhaps stunting in its own way considering the demands that come with any prestigious work.

Demands as well as the razor-thin edge my reputation would be balanced on, I suspect. The wrong move, however small, would likely result in a stained name that'll likely spread from court to court like a plague. At any rate, I'd reassured Signor Cloutier that I was—and still am—very comfortable where I am despite the persistent shadow of poverty hanging over my head and threatening my days if Mamma's strictures on economy weren't followed.

*

23 April, 17—The study beside the music room is now Signor Amatore's home office, if you will. Furniture has been moved around (much to my pupil's excitement) so that the harpsichord stands in the middle of the music room and not off to one corner. It's also been turned a bit so that Maddalena and I are somewhat at an angle facing the generously sized windows and the afternoon sunlight streaming through them. How very theatrical!

As for my employer, Signor Amatore has also made a few changes in the study, moving his writing-table (not desk, mind!) to the middle of the room with the chair facing the double doors connecting the study to the music room.

"I'd like to listen to your music without any impediments," he said with a pleased grin as he inspected his servants' handiwork. "While Maddalena practices, I'll keep the doors open so I can see her. Rest assured, signore, I won't intrude no matter what. If she falters or makes mistakes, you won't hear a thing from me."

He pressed a finger against his lips and actually winked at me—a playful and unexpected gesture that left me blinking for a moment, but there was nothing but jovial relief in him.

To be sure, it looked as though he'd just had a great weight lifted off his shoulders, and he was suddenly feeling like a careless youth all over again, for which I'm grateful. His decision to stay home, which I suspect wasn't an easy thing to do considering the demands of a successful business requiring his presence and his hand in everything, has brightened my pupil's world considerably.

And I couldn't help but approach Signor Amatore at the end of today's lesson and thank him sincerely. He appeared surprised but quickly eased into pleasure, and he merely shook my hand and—to my shock—dropped a kiss to my knuckles before shaking it again and then releasing it. Tears gathered in his eyes as he shook his head.

"No, signore. The gratitude is entirely mine," he replied, blinking away the moisture. "I've never been an affectionate father to my child, but having you come and help her find her voice, so to speak, and encourage her to sing to God with such beautiful music? I've been brought down to earth and humbled by your patience and affection for my poor daughter, the results of which I'm now bearing witness to day after day. Thank you."

He actually said a lot more, but those were all the words I could remember because he'd caught me completely off-guard, and I couldn't do much more than stare, owl-like, at the gentleman while he praised me with so many flattering and tearfully spoken words. If he claimed to be humbled, so did I. Indeed, I never once thought myself to be a savior of any kind, but I seemed to have taken on such a heavy mantle.

All the same, I can't say it wasn't flattering to be praised so generously and in my face at that. It also helps me redouble my efforts and ensure Maddalena's lessons are thorough and well-planned beforehand. My pupil's progress has steadily picked up speed, which reflects her confidence. I don't think I've heard her say a single critical word about her physical limitations for a good while now, and she's been holding herself up with a straighter bearing as befits a gentleman's daughter. Everything's looking wonderfully promising!

*

25 April, 17—The older Cloutier finally returned home from his recent shorter travels. Or, I meant Jori's older brother (or half-brother), Gilles. I confess it's rather funny seeing the two together because regardless of their age difference, they're very much mirror images of each other. I sincerely doubt if their mothers had anything to do with their overly somber manner, but perhaps something in their paternal bloodline ensures young men of a particular quality: dignified, withdrawn, and thoughtful academics.

Gilles is also quite worldly in spite of his restraint, and all one needs to do is encourage him to talk about anything else *but* the family business. His mood lifts the way clouds break apart, allowing brilliant sunlight through, and he becomes quite the chatterbox.

And it didn't take me long to discover he's very much a connoisseur of art, music, and literature, heavily favoring visual art. I suppose that makes a lot of sense since his business is dependent upon interior design and everything that's fashionable—beautiful and extravagant for today's wealthy patrons.

Once he's encouraged to talk about what he's seen in salons or drawing-rooms or whatnot, his mood changes considerably, and his pale, patrician features suddenly glow and shed a few years. It stirs a good deal of fond delight in the senior Cloutier, who's quite content to sit back and let his grandson lead the conversation.

"Perhaps you can show our young tutor here some of the places you're helping beautify," Signor Cloutier piped up during a pause in conversation. "Gilles here has been lucky enough to catch the attention of a couple of aristocrats, you know. One owns a palazzo in Venice, and the other's in Naples, and both boast some of the grandest and most ostentatious interiors weighed down with art. Perhaps arrangements can be made for you to see either one or both places if Gilles is willing to share his passion with our M. Agnelli. God knows the boy needs to go out and enjoy the world a little more."

I didn't know if he was referring to Gilles or to me in that final sentence, but regardless of whom, I thought it was rather funny and held back my laughter. I first thought Gilles would take exception to his grandfather's sudden meddling, but he seemed to welcome the suggestion as though suddenly realizing that, yes, he was very much in charge of his own time.

Just like Signor Amatore was now reclaiming his hours, I thought, though Gilles was certainly not as passionate and handsome as the other gentleman even if he's perhaps fifteen years Signor Amatore's junior.

Chapter 7

I barely made it through my finals, and somehow I managed to keep my grades up. With the summer break now on, I decided not to register for classes as I needed to get my shit together first. I figured then it would be good for me to just focus on work and catch up on sleep for the rest of the day, every day, until the start of the Fall term. Even my advisor noticed the shadows under my eyes and had been digging around for answers—pretty subtly, at least, but I instantly recognized where she was trying to go.

I told her a while ago that I was planning to transfer to a state university after I got all my core classes out of the way, but the more I lost my hold on my sleep, the less confident I got. My momentum had been derailed a little by my lack of proper rest even if I still managed to ace my classes.

"You might as well be a prodigy, Adam, the way you just breeze through academics," Mom said when I showed her my final grades. Then she waved a hand when I opened my mouth to correct her. "I know, I know, prodigies mean something else, but what other word can I use to describe your success in school?"

Hard working, I guess? That would be two words, though, and I knew better than to counter her belief in God-given natural gifts trumping dedication, discipline, and honest-to-goodness hard work. I suppose in that sense I was old-fashioned, but I did bust my butt in my studies since I was a kid. If anything was God-given about me, it'd be my nerd-dom when it came to school—as well as my uncanny ability to stay under my classmates' radar while kicking their asses academically.

I hated drama. I hated being noticed. I wanted, more than anything else, to be left alone so I could get the job done, whether in school or otherwise. I realized it was maybe a pretty strange attitude for someone my age to have since teenagers were hardwired for risk and experimentation as a way of learning more about the world and themselves. Not me, though.

And while I sometimes caught myself watching my classmates and friends—of whom there were less than a handful through high school, and we were never really that close—with a pang of envy and regret, I regarded their embrace of life with mild horror.

"You sound like an old man," Ms. Garza once said with a puzzled frown while staring at me as though I were some weird specimen from someone's Biology Lab experiment. "What do you do for fun, then, if you don't look for it with friends?"

"I read a lot," I replied with an indignant huff. "Not just online stuff, but books—like real, physical books from the library and stuff."

"Huh. Sure."

Maybe my negative visceral response to attention was a symptom of some psychiatric disorder, but at least my parents approved of it and even considered it a plus since it meant I wasn't going to cause any problems for them. I was a proper Catholic boy, I suppose, and life in the Sheridan household went on.

* * * *

I woke up to rain—a freak weather pattern, I think, since summer was finally here, but I wasn't one to complain. I loved rain and sometimes wished we could move to a state that had four seasons, not one (perpetual sun and only varying temps and fog presence).

That said, I'd take what I could get, and it also helped I didn't have a restless night. Fully recharged and relaxed, I fed myself breakfast since Mom and Dad had gone off to work and left me a note about food and got ready to go to work, myself.

The warehouse wasn't that far—about a twenty-minute walk from home, which I didn't mind doing since it grounded me and allowed me to lose myself in my head while being active. I had to walk past a few blocks of old buildings that had been turned into street-level shops with apartments above them. Narrow, dingy alleys were common, and I normally glanced down their way when I passed for safety's sake.

I was about halfway to the warehouse when the clouds really went for broke and sent us a full-on deluge. People who were trying to get around on foot yelped, and even with their umbrellas, they risked their necks by picking up speed to get the hell out of the rain. I tried to avoid them—naturally—though it was also my instinct to get indoors ASAP and therefore slowed my pace, grateful for the extra-wide umbrella my dad foisted on me a couple of years ago.

I passed the corner coffee shop, the real estate office next door, and the bath shop next to that, my attention now fully on the sidewalk and the people frantically making their way from point A to B. The narrow blind alley came next, and I stepped onto the next half-block before stopping dead, blinking.

"Wait," I muttered, looking around me. "Was there..."

I looked back, my gaze following the sidewalk I'd just covered and the short gap marking the entrance to the alley before the rest of the sidewalk leading to the corner coffee shop. Did something just happen? No—was something different back there?

I slowly turned around and doubled back, my pace slow and careful, my eyes moving restlessly as I visually mapped an area that was an established part of my usual route to and from work as well as school. I could walk down that specific block without even thinking about it—even with my eyes shut—and still know what was what or what was where.

Every time I crossed that short gap of the alley's entrance, I barely gave the narrow, dead-end space a glance since it was nothing more than three brick walls filled with graffiti and grime, a couple of dumpsters standing against opposite walls. Sometimes those dumpsters just reeked of garbage, especially when the weather was hot, and I was also used to the stench.

When I paused at the blind alley's entrance and stared down the short space, I saw nothing different.

But something in me—something deep down—wasn't going to be satisfied with the obvious proof of nothing being suddenly different. I doubled back to the coffee shop, looked around, and then sighed as I resumed my walk, again passing the alley and sparing it another confused look.

Something had been different, my gut told me. Something had changed.

There *had* been something there one moment, but it wasn't there now.

And whatever it was had been in that blind alley, specifically near or at the farthest end of it—the farthest wall. But whatever it might have been didn't register more clearly enough in my gut to give me a better idea of what it might be. Somehow the first thing coming to mind was a man, standing and watching, silent and sad. I didn't know why, but there it was.

I grimaced as I walked on, wondering if I was just hallucinating and, if so, maybe it meant those restless nights were going to make themselves felt in more than one way.

Once I got to the warehouse, though, all those questions and troubling ideas quickly flew out of my head because Christian was there, clocking in at the same time I did, and he immediately smiled and waved when he saw me. He even said "good morning" in that voice of his—so low and pleasant but strangely still easily heard in the midst of all the noise of the machines in the back.

And with the steady drumming of the rain against the roof, I found myself relaxing and easily sinking into a happy haze as I took my place at my workstation, my gaze flicking several times at Christian's back, sometimes tracking his movements whenever he brought his completed frames to the cart, which he wheeled to the other side of the warehouse for inventory and packaging.

I admit it was pretty hard not to appear stupid avoiding his gaze whenever he looked my way. In fact, I couldn't figure out how best to behave like a normal (uninterested) person whenever he was around, and to an extent I was a bit miffed that we spent our shifts with his back to me for a good part of the day. That said, I was able to stare at him without shame and catalog my own visual inventory of him, which was pretty impressive.

He was a little taller than me, and I stood at five-foot-ten. He was bigger boned and healthier-looking in terms of coloring since his complexion always made it seem as though he spent a good part of his time outdoors, but he told me once he was biracial, half of his relatives hailing from Mexico though he was born and raised in the U.S. His hair—cropped really short on the sides and back and longer on the top—looked so soft and fine, and he seemed to be too aware of it since he constantly raked his fingers through, and it was all I could do to gawk at the way the straight strands fell airily into place.

Really, I sound like a real piece of work by describing him that way, but I couldn't help take all those details in. It was pretty obvious I was crushing seriously on Christian, and when I saw he also wore a few bracelets—a couple of really narrow, rainbow-colored friendship bracelets in the mix, at that—my heart skipped a beat.

That day, he shed his thick hoodie and revealed a black t-shirt with a small pride logo or patch on the upper-left part of the chest, and I could've danced at my workstation.

I didn't own anything with a pride logo or something indicating I was gay because while my parents were tolerant enough, they specifically told me not to brag about it or go off and flaunt my "lifestyle" seeing as how that would only endanger me in some cases, and in others, well—it wasn't a good thing to flaunt something that could very well be a phase I was going through, was it?

Tattoos were out. Jewelry save my wristwatch was out. Wearing certain hairstyles was out.

I suppose being born risk-averse really played well into my family's philosophy and especially religion, but with my new job and Christian being there, I was beginning to rethink my turn toward avoidance and invisibility. In fact, by the second week of working there, I mustered up enough courage to approach him casually though my heart palpitated, and I could barely breathe.

"Oh, I didn't know you're into Marvel," I stammered, nodding at a DVD of the first *Avengers* film. He'd just pulled it out of his backpack and set it aside in order to rummage through his stuff. "Have you seen the newest movie yet? I think it's been out for a week."

He beamed then and got into full nerd mode, and I loved it.

Chapter 8

28 April, 17—Papà received some wonderful news today regarding a new commission, and it's a large one. Word has gotten around about his skill in beautifying homes with frescoes ("vanity frescoes" as he always calls them), and now representatives of wealthy families are reaching out to him with questions. This one is in Venice—in one of those palazzos people keep talking up to me as if I was interested to live in one. Clearly no one knows me at all, but that's all right.

"Surely you should hire at least a couple of people to help you," I said over dinner, both delighted and aghast. "You can't just take on a palazzo on your own, Papà."

"I'm looking into that, of course, but talks are still in progress with this new commission, and my decision will depend on what more I can learn about the project. That said, Paolo, this will bring in so much money, and we won't have to hold back so much on essentials," he replied, his eyes alit with excitement and joy over the prospects. "You might even want to travel a little and learn more about your favorite masters, bring home books or sheet music of their best works for the harpsichord. That should make you even more attractive to potential employers, surely."

I had to smile at him—my ever-devoted, ever-loving father who still thinks the world of me in spite of my limited prospects. I suppose he understands well enough about the barriers I constantly face. I've glimpsed that occasional shadow dimming his eyes when I used to talk about Couperin, Albinoni, Marais, Scarlatti...

He understood well enough, and I love him and Mamma—their zeal, their sacrifices over the years on my account—more than anything. I do have my age going for me, I'll admit, and I can easily boast of being the youngest private music tutor in this region, at least. Bless Signor Belluomo and his connections, for he got me started on my journey, even bequeathing all of his books and lessons to me. I hope I'm doing him justice.

"Not only that, son," Papà said after a moment's comfortable pause. "There might be a possible restoration or clean-up job in a small church, just outside Venice. If I do get hired for it, I can easily travel back and forth."

He also indicated that the palazzo commission might require us to move to Venice, which was the only shadow darkening our dinner. Moving to Venice means giving up my work here, and I really don't want to do that. There's time enough to discuss things further, and Papà did say he'll also make sure I'll not be forced to sacrifice so much of my work for him. Perhaps a compromise won't be too difficult to reach since Venice isn't too far to travel to, and he may be the only one to move there until the commission's done.

I really hope things work out for both of us.

*

2 May, 17—I find that I'm enjoying Gilles's company, which is astonishing since I've never been one to connect so easily with the more gregarious and energetic members of society. However, this side of him comes out only when he's in very select company: family and very close friends, of whom he has a mere handful. Not that he's an utter bastard, but he's excessively fussy and selective when it comes to his inner circle.

I'm honored to be considered his friend.

It also helps that his presence at home lifts his younger brother's spirits, and Jori goes through his exercises with an energy that almost seems foreign. Granted, the boy's still very much the quiet and serious child I'm growing very fond of, but what he's unable to express in conversation or simply face-to-face interaction, he easily lets out through music.

And his skills are improving at an astounding rate—probably because his focus is almost unnatural in someone so young. In fact, I can't think of a moment when he behaved like a normal child or even like Maddalena, who's still prone to distraction and childish fancy.

At any rate, Gilles and his grandfather entertained me with such happy conversation after Jori's lessons, and I was obliged to linger a little longer until lunch was served, and they convinced me to stay and eat with the family.

And the conversation naturally gravitated toward the dining-room, where things carried on as though we weren't momentarily interrupted by the move. Jori appeared surprised at having me over for lunch at first but then eased into a shy but happy young boy who was content to just eat and listen to the adults around him.

Gilles also managed to convince me to accompany him to a villa he's been hired to beautify with some exquisite marquetry.

"This is a quick job, really," he said in his perfect Italian. "I'm to design some furniture for the villa, not the actual floors. It's something a friend of a friend brought to my attention."

"But you've got the other larger commissions in Naples and Venice," I replied, eyes bulging.

"I won't be torn into a dozen different directions all at once. I'm only there to come up with ideas, perfect the design, get approval—and an initial payment, of course—and my craftsmen will take care of the rest."

So easy, I thought, my mind going back to Papà and how *he* took care of business. One artisan with enviable skill and talent—that's always been his way. The more I listened to Gilles and learned more about his approach to business, the more I realized Papà would someday require extra pairs of hands since he isn't getting any younger, and frescoes really are the only thing that truly makes him happy.

But, I suppose, there goes the chasm-wide difference between people with money and those without.

Gilles and I are set to visit this villa tomorrow, which is perfect since the Amatore family is out visiting relatives this week, and I'll have more free time to rest and catch up on some long-neglected housework.

*

3 May, 17—I'm exhausted! The visit to that villa in Verona took us all day, but it was time well-spent as I've never been anywhere beyond Padova. Gilles was in his element, meeting and conversing with the gentleman who's intent upon turning up the sparkle of his property for his new bride. I shadowed them like a faithful puppy, which was how I reckon I appeared to everyone there, but to Gilles's credit, he never let me out of his sight. He even introduced me as a "talented" music tutor to just about everyone who cared to hear about me.

"That's to plant a seed in their heads just in case someone's child begs for lessons," Gilles confided in me with a sly grin and a twinkle in his eye when we were left alone for a moment.

"It's a long way to travel for lessons," I muttered back. "I don't think I can afford to hire a horse or any proper conveyance."

But he merely patted my arm as though it wasn't something worth considering, which is quite normal for someone in his position. "Seeds can be carried across great distances, my friend. If I said something here, there's a chance someone elsewhere will hear about you, and that elsewhere will be a much more desirable distance for you."

I'll admit I had to laugh at his ease and carelessness, and it was all I could do to shake my head just when our host returned with his manager, and Gilles let the curtain of business and very serious talk fall back into place. We were given a tour of the villa, with the gentleman—a Signor Bassanelli—showing us his extensive collection of art.

"He and I met in Paris, you know," Gilles said as we followed our host through a gallery. "We share the same taste in art."

Signor Bassanelli, who appeared to be in his fifties, laughed, and the early restraint and stiffness were gone in a breath once their art adventures became our topic of conversation. Well, *their* topic of conversation, at any rate, since I had nothing to contribute other than a very eager ear and a mouth that stayed silent but hung loosely in awe at the magnificent paintings I was seeing.

They'd traveled extensively in both France and Italy, and Signor Bassanelli was especially knowledgeable of great artists and their influences. He said his favorite French artist is Nicolas Poussin, whose commissioned painting for a pope introduced our host to a particular genre of art: *vanitas*. I'm familiar with such a subject in art since I've seen a few lesser works in a couple of homes where I used to teach, and they've always been a sobering reminder of the futility of material acquisition and so on.

But this painting done by Signor Poussin, which both our host and Gilles had seen and marveled over, was unique in its treatment of death in life. Or death even in an idyll. They proceeded to describe the painting in such detail that I could see it in my head, and when Gilles made a quick and rough sketch of the piece, every element fell into place and matched what I'd managed to conjure in my mind. It was astonishing, and I heartily wished I could see it.

Indeed, both gentlemen talked about the painting so much that my ignorant self couldn't help but devour every word and make it mine, the tranquil and yet slightly unsettling pastoral scene firmly turning into a fixture in my head. Mamma would have urged me never to forget because it's a very important lesson meant to humble a man. Beauty and happiness might surround us day after day, but nothing's forever. Life, especially, is ephemeral at best.

That said, I went through the entire visit lost in both wonder and amusement because Signor Bassanelli still appeared to value material things above all else despite his love for Signor Poussin's work. Here and there, no money was spared in his acquisition of whatever he fancied, and now he was about to get married and was determined to present his new bride this magnificent villa and the treasures it holds.

We enjoyed a delicious lunch at our host's insistence, and by one o'clock, we were ready to go. Gilles spent a few more moments in conversation with Signor Bassanelli, finalizing the commission and the terms, but I can't say much more about it since all that was done behind closed doors, and I was left to gape stupidly at the villa's well-kept and gorgeously designed gardens.

"Signor Bassanelli's bride must be the luckiest woman alive," I said once we were safely in our coach.

"Indeed she is," Gilles replied with a smirk. "Our friend's fifty-two, and the lady's your age. Mark that, monsieur."

He laughed nearly all the way back home because I suspect I must have stared at him with the most ridiculous look on my face. Anyway, the hour's late, and my wrist's screaming at me. If Mamma were around, she'd scold me for risking injury on my hand—my "blessed" hand, according to her.

Chapter 9

Another week passed fairly uneventfully though I'd woken up sobbing into my pillow without remembering why in the middle of the night a couple of times, at least. My heart hurt so badly each time, and my brain felt sunk in a puddle of sludge I had a hard time surfacing from. I didn't want to see a shrink. I was absolutely terrified of that possibility, but the more this happened, the higher the chance got.

My parents had signed up for a month-long prayer retreat, which was a tradition they strictly followed every year. When I was little, they left me with my grandparents, who were way worse as devout Catholics, but at least I didn't know I was gay back then, and their main complaint about me was that I "read too many books" and "didn't play enough". I did pray with them, however, so they didn't make life hell for me.

When I was older, I still stayed with my grandparents—mostly my grandmother since Grandpa was already gone by then. Nothing changed, but I at least helped her with chores, and conversation wasn't as stilted as it had been with Grandpa hovering around us. Grandma died about five years ago, and Mom and Dad reduced their time at the retreat to just two weeks since I was left alone in the house save for our neighbor, who'd come around to check up on me as a massive favor to my parents.

Since I'm now eighteen, Mom and Dad could go back to their month-long thing without having to worry about me. This time I'd managed to convince them to have Ms. Garza come by every now and then to check up on me since she and I had grown very close, and I now regarded her like a second grandmother.

"Adam, here's the retreat's contact information," Mom said as she scurried around to make sure everything was good to go. "We all have to give up our phones when we get there, but families can still reach us through the main office. They're pretty quick in finding participants whenever calls go through, but only call them when it's urgent, okay?"

I nodded. "Okay, Mom. Don't worry. I know the drill."

"I know, sweetheart. Now be good, all right? Don't give Socorro any reason to cuss you out in Spanish."

I had to laugh. Ms. Garza cusses at me and around me in Spanish all the time since I loved pulling her strings a lot. *No seas pendejo!* I'd already memorized that phrase, which she'd say to me with a roll of her eyes at least once each time we're together. In fact, she knew just how much I loved the word *pendejo* though I'd yet to use it on something or someone.

"Do you have your rosary? Prayer book? Prayer journal?"

"Yes, yes, and yes. Thank you, honey." Mom grinned and hugged me, kissing my cheek when she pulled away. "Behave yourself. I know you're old enough to know better, and I trust you, but I don't trust the rest of the world. Don't cave to temptation, no matter how good it looks." She paused and hesitated, looking a little uncomfortable. "How handsome or hot it looks."

"I promise." Clearly she still had a hard time acknowledging my gayness and couldn't wrap her mind around warnings involving the same gender. She'd have had a way easier time saying "how pretty or hot it looks".

By eight o'clock that morning, I was all alone in the house, and I didn't quite know what to do with myself. I wanted to take a nap to make up for another night of troubled sleep, but the thought of falling asleep again made my skin crawl, and my gut didn't feel good.

I snatched my keys and shrugged on my jacket without a plan in my head. All I knew then was that I needed to stay awake and move around a little—get out of the house while the weather allowed it. The freak weather system stuck around, and while the rain stopped for now, the clouds were growing darker and heavier by the minute. Maybe being caught in the rain would be good for me, I thought.

I just wandered around, window-shopping now and then without a real purpose and without really liking anything I saw. I had ants in my pants, and I just had to get out. Anyone who was superstitious would probably warn me against going out—bad weather notwithstanding—and for me to just suck it up and stick around at home, distracting myself with bad food and endless bingeing in front of my computer.

The sky opened up and puked before long, and I was the only stupid one walking around without an umbrella, so this time around, everyone still outside just snapped their umbrellas open and kept going without a pause in their stride. I, on the other hand, practically threw myself against a wall under an overhang, blinking and looking like a total idiot.

I didn't even know where I was since I wasn't paying too much attention and simply turned one corner after another or crossed intersections without checking the street names. I tried not to hear Ms. Garza's snarky voice in my head and *pendejo* tap dancing all over my consciousness as I zipped up my jacket, wrapped my arms tightly around myself, and stalked off to—wherever. Not home, though. I didn't want to go home in spite of everything.

A couple of minutes passed before the rain turned into a solid downpour to the point where earthbound water looked more like a solid wall than a natural phenomenon. People carrying umbrellas now had no choice but to hurry along, some crying out in surprise or dismay as they tried to get the hell out of the rain's way.

I even bumped into another person—a blond guy about my age—who stammered "I'm sorry" and stepped aside, his blue eyes wide and startled. Familiar, even, but I hurried past him.

I ran in spite of the danger of slipping and cracking my head open, and with my eyes squinted against the rain, I barely managed to spot the open door to San Tadeo church as well as someone disappearing inside, likely in the same situation as me.

Just a quick movement in the shadows within, but it didn't matter at that point, and I suspected my parents would have something to say about the timing of the rain and the fact that I found myself in the vicinity of San Tadeo church when that happened.

I ran up the low adobe steps, my hand barely gripping the wet rail, my head bowed against the downpour. When I got up to the church entrance, I found the doors shut and nearly went splat against the thick wood like some cartoon character.

I stood there, blinking and staring, wondering what the hell I just saw, and when I tested the doors, I found them locked. The sign to the right of the entrance noted the church was closed on this day of the week, but I could have sworn the doors were open. There was even someone going inside. I was sure of it.

But San Tadeo church was closed, sure enough, and I was so confused and miserable standing in front of the double doors, staring at them as though just doing that would somehow unlock them completely. And since there was no overhang or awnings I could take advantage of, I had to turn around and walk back, forcing my feet in the direction of my house.

"God, I'm hallucinating now. I don't know what's happening," I muttered, glancing back to make sure the church was closed, and it was.

I was back home eventually, looking like a complete wreck, and feeling more and more terrified for my sake. I didn't want to go crazy. I didn't want to be locked away. I took a hot shower, had brunch, and felt relaxed and tired enough to stretch out on the sofa with one of Grandma's crocheted throws on top of me, and the steady rain outside lulled me to sleep. *Oh, God, here I go again,* I thought, dismayed, as I drifted off.

I'd barely closed my eyes when I found myself in that same dark, unknown church again, that horrible side chapel some distance away and still empty, but this time I was standing in the middle aisle and watching someone pray several pews away. The church was dark and cold, and only a few candles were lit, so I couldn't really make out more details then. The silence was eerie and completely unsettling, making me feel more and more like I was in a place that was completely real and yet detached from time in some inexplicable way.

The person praying was male—a young man. I couldn't see his face, and I only had a view of his back and his bowed head, but I was convinced he was young.

He prayed, his soft voice sometimes making itself heard in the chilly silence of the church, but I couldn't make out any words. His voice rose and fell, rose and fell, and I wondered if he was praying the rosary since there seemed to be a cadence to his murmuring—as though he were repeating phrases as one would the rosary's decades.

In fact, that cadence seemed to calm me, a soothing rhythm whose repetition felt like gentle strokes easing my nervousness and simmering fear.

In another moment, I was just watching him pray with a small lump in my throat though I still didn't know why I was there or why I was affected that way by a vision. Maybe it was the silent church itself. Maybe the side chapel and the heavy, crippling sadness that was associated with it. Or maybe there was something in that solitary figure that found some weird connection with me at a deep, unreachable level.

I couldn't help but take a few quiet and cautious steps closer, my eyes never leaving him, and the less distance between us, the more I saw he was dressed in really old fashion—the same clothes I'd seen in history books or shows. Not from the time when people wore wigs and all kinds of lacy stuff, but the darker and simpler style that was common in the nineteenth century. His hair was dark and short, with lots of waves that barely gleamed in the shadowy church.

His prayers continued as though he weren't aware of my presence, and I saw his pale hands clasping each other so tightly they were actually shaking. His head was bowed, and he kept murmuring, but once I was close enough, his prayer stuttered and his shoulders shook, and I knew he was praying and sobbing at the same time. I stopped, gawking, but something held me back and forced me to watch someone's heart break in a really bad way.

Why me? What have I done? Why can't you take it away?

I reared back, shocked now, because I understood every word even though it all came out in German. And what was even more shocking was the fact that I recognized those words deep down—recognized them because I was sure I'd said them myself. I jerked awake to an empty house and what felt like endless rain outside.

Chapter 10

7 May, 17—Signor Amatore's decision to spend more time at home and in his daughter's company is proving to be a wise one. Maddalena's taken to behaving herself like a proper little adult though she does slip every so often and respond with childish excitement or petulance when I say something complimentary or sternly.

The spring season has been a blessing all in all though tainted by Mamma's passing. In truth, even with the sudden change in our situation, Papà and I are doing quite well and are managing to save a little more money so that we can treat ourselves to small luxuries (mostly food).

Signor Amatore has increased my pay, much to my amazement, and he said it was because of the unexpected improvements I've made in Maddalena's behavior and outlook. She's always been a very sweet and affectionate child, but the loss of her mother and her father's neglect have dimmed her light for too long. Music's been her saving grace, and while her enthusiasm for it has always been there, it's shed even more of its cloak when her father realized his blunder and resolved to stick around the house for her sake.

"Business has never been better, signore," he said today after the lesson, and Maddalena was once again led away by one of the servants for washing. Signor Amatore invited me to the sitting-room, where he had a tray of coffee and baked goods sent. "I've rearranged my schedule some more to spend my mornings at the workshop and oversee my little army of ceramic heroes. Half a day at work is better than nothing, and I can keep an eye on the flow of production and fulfillment of orders."

Of which his company—a surprisingly small one considering its success—has enjoyed what feels like an endless surge, according to him. His passion for centuries-old ceramics, maiolica in particular, has led him down a long and winding road to success, and he never tires of bragging about his impoverished roots and his stunning rise to success as one of the finest purveyors of handmade ceramics in Italy.

He invited me to have dinner with the family, but I had to decline. He was quite enthusiastic about the coffee and small cakes he'd especially had made for me, apparently, for which I was not only grateful but also flattered speechless. I can't remember what the cakes were called now, which says a lot about my state of mind at that moment, when he admitted it all.

They did taste divine, and Signor Amatore described them as something ridiculously dramatic as "flowers for an angel" while pinning me in my seat with a very heavy and bright-eyed look. I swear my face must have turned redder than a tomato, and I suppose it only means I really should be able to take flattering attention more gamely.

*

12 May, 17—Maddalena showed off to her father today, which was a delightful scene, yet I couldn't help but feel a little unfocused and confused at first. Perhaps it's overwork though I really can't see things that way since, compared to Papà's more backbreaking work spent in longer and more torturous hours, I'm quite drowning in luxury.

Had the families I've been working with paid me less, I'd be tutoring maybe close to a dozen pupils from sunrise to sundown, day after day. But I've been fortunate and blessed with the compensation I've been receiving from the people whose attention I've attracted.

Today ought to have been a very good day all in all, but I felt a little ill at ease the whole time. It started, I think, when I entered the Amatore house, and something felt a little off, but of course I couldn't prove it to myself and dismissed it readily enough as nothing more than a symptom of possible fatigue.

Maddalena went through her scales beautifully and proceeded to play a short French piece I'd chosen specifically to show off her improved dexterity and grace. She performed it with a confidence of a young lady intent upon conquering the world with the most exquisite music ever written, and I was quite proud of her.

She sat at the harpsichord while I stood a bit of a distance to allow her privacy and space. The double doors to her father's study were thrown wide open, and Signor Amatore sat at his desk with his letters and other writing tasks, facing the music room. All that time I'd been watching my pupil, my gaze unwavering and determined as I watched her hands and willed them to do this or do that, responding as a devoted tutor would whenever his pupil succeeded or faltered in places.

Somewhere halfway through the scales, I glanced up and found Signor Amatore leaning back in his chair—not watching his daughter but watching *me*. His gaze was intent, thoughtful, and even bold, and I didn't know what to make of it. I had to incline my head a little in respectful acknowledgment, which he didn't respond to, before turning my attention back to my pupil.

It was a good thing Maddalena kept my attention throughout the lesson, or I wouldn't have known what to do with myself beside perhaps springing behind a potted plant and hiding from my employer's view—which I felt like a subtle weight on me once I saw his interest was on me and not his daughter. As it tended to happen, when one's awareness of something odd has been triggered, he can't help but be drawn to it despite gut instinct, and I wasn't immune.

Now and then I'd happen to look up, and my gaze would always stray to him—only to find him still watching me intently, this time with a small smile on his face, and I had to look away. The faint unease I felt upon entering the house earlier strengthened, but I had to shake it off and force myself to keep my mind on my pupil. I was being paid handsomely now for her improvement, and the least I could do for the family is to see to my end of the bargain.

Signor Amatore congratulated us both after the lesson, kissing Maddalena on both cheeks and praising her skills, which the girl took in with such open happiness so rarely seen in her when we first worked together. When the servant came in and took her away, I had to decline coffee and cakes because Papà needed me to go by the apothecary for some pain-easing medicine, and I didn't want to tarry with his physical troubles currently slowing him down.

"Ah, how unfortunate," Signor Amatore said with a regretful air. "Perhaps next time, then."

It was only at the apothecary when I realized he hadn't said anything else about Maddalena's progress besides the congratulations for a "good performance" and the praise for "increasingly nimble fingers". My pupil took that with such childish pleasure that I never even gave the mediocre acclaim (if such were a thing) any thought until well after the moment.

I don't like feeling ungrateful or uncharitable toward Signor Amatore, who's already increased my pay and done so much for me and my family, but I can't help it, and I particularly don't like retiring from the day feeling this sourness in my belly.

*

15 May, 17—Papà's very ill, and it's worrying me. He's been rolling his eyes at my panicked questions and impatient suggestions for a physician, saying, "I'm not an immortal, Paolo. I'm not getting any younger, either. I need rest and some proper food, and that's all."

I'm not convinced! I don't know what I'd do if something really dire were to happen to him, but such a thought shouldn't even be entertained if I want him to get better. His joints ache, and he has a fever, and one of the friars who came by to see to his care with some medicine claimed he's been overworked and that it's his fault entirely (Brother Rafael never minces words, seeing as how he and Papà have been friends since the beginning of time).

Papà, on the other hand, actually made a rude sound at Brother Rafael with his tongue sticking out of his mouth, which left me gaping in horror and the friar laughing hard.

All the same, Papà's condition worries me, especially now that I'm also wondering if continuing my work at the Amatore household is worth the growing nervousness I'm feeling around Signor Amatore.

I dare not speak a word to it to Papà because, really, I've nothing solid to present as proof. A reason to quit what's now my highest-paying employment? I've got nothing.

Today was the same as before: a good deal of unashamed watching from my employer while his daughter's once again neglected in his presence. Considering how dependent I am on Signor Amatore's generosity, I couldn't find it in myself to hide or do something to dissuade him from this strange fascination he now has in me.

I don't even know *why* I'd attract his attention like this. I do find him awfully handsome for a man his age, and I've always been inclined toward the male sex when I'm faced with a room of beautiful people.

I've never given my parents a reason to worry about my character somehow endangering girls around me though they've never suspected a thing about my preferences. I'd like to keep things that way with Papà until the day I lose him. He's been through enough already, and shocking him with my nature now will likely drive him to a passionate rage.

If Papà's unable to return to work because of this illness, I'll be well and fully trapped. I'll have to hold on to what I have with the Amatore and Cloutier families given their generosity with my pay, and I'll need to add to their numbers with other families, but those tend to be few and far between unless I travel, which is another expense I can't afford. If worse comes to worst, I'll find work at a shop or something—wherever my limited prospects fit, I suppose, and that's rather alarming. Besides music, what else can I offer?

I don't like writing nothing but negativity in my journal; however, that's how my week's been progressing in spite of my pupils' improvements. At least Jori and his family haven't given me anything to fret over though Gilles is once more away on business, and his poor brother's back to being the quiet and shy genius who's stolen my heart.

Maddalena continues to be wholly unaware of her father's gradual return to indifference toward her now that he's begun to entertain this ludicrous idea that I'm somehow worth his time. Today and yesterday he once again invited me to have coffee and cakes with him in the sitting-room, and I had to decline, but at least I had Papà's illness for my excuse. Signor Amatore took my refusals with good enough humor, but I thought I saw a tightness in his smile today, but that might be just my confusion and unease playing tricks on me.

I tried to pray to the Virgin on my way home, stopping by the church, but my heart remains troubled, and I can't settle down.

Chapter 11

The freak weather storm turned even freakier the following day, this time the rain easing up for now but leaving a really thick fog behind. News stations said nothing new but the obvious—that, yep, we were in a for this unusual weather system coming in from the northwest as though Winter decided to liven things up a little and to troll Summer.

Mom and Dad checked up on me last night, and everything was good with them. They were only too happy to go back to a full month's worth of prayers, meditation, socializing, and just plain relaxation away from their responsibilities. They earned it, really, and I desperately needed the space even though their distance from me seemed to stoke their paranoia a little. Too many conservative Catholics around them feeding their suspicious minds with stuff, too little space to move, which meant I was going to be screwed eventually.

At work, I showed up like some horror movie reject though a couple of the custom framers gave me a thumbs up and said I looked like a well-dressed emo vampire. I saw my reflection in the mirror of one of the restrooms at work and had to laugh. My skin had gone even paler if that were even possible, but my restless nights in bed also stamped my face with shadows under my eyes and slightly bloodshot eyeballs. I had to make use of those eye drops from the company's massive first aid cabinet to make myself look less bloodthirsty.

That day a new guy showed up and was given the workstation behind me. His name was Elliot, and the three of us together made a "spectrum" of "YA love interests", according to Jodie, who was the manager of our side of the warehouse.

Christian was the tall, pretty, polite overachiever; I was the tall, lanky, brooding outsider; Elliot was the short, cute, mousy intellectual with his glasses, braces, and shy smile. All of us were also either in their last year of high school (Elliot) and their first year in college (me and Christian), and at least for the summer, we all worked more or less full-time. I learned Elliot was a seasonal employee, which explained why he knew what needed to be done right away.

It hadn't taken me long to get the hang of what I did, and while it was repetitive and even boring in parts, I at least had my music to keep me going, and it really helped me keep my mind focused and avoid accidentally slicing myself with glass or shooting myself with a tab gun. Having Christian work in front and occasionally moving around his table so that he worked facing me helped, too. Every now and then we'd both look up and lock gazes, and he'd smile while I tried a pretty weak mirror of it.

Every now and then he'd walk past my table to check on Elliot, who was apparently one of the most efficient and dependable workers because I'd see him frequently marching past my table pushing a fully loaded cart of frames he'd just finished to the shrinkwrap corner for final packaging. In my case, by the time I'd have one cart loaded, he'd have filled his cart twice.

Christian was like the unspoken supervisor who answered to Jodie whenever she came by to check on everyone, and she'd always go to him first for a full rundown on our progress before stopping by our individual workstations for a quick one-to-one. She was a doting older sister to everyone, the polar opposite of overly caffeinated and jittery David, the manager of the custom framing side.

I couldn't get over just beautiful Christian was, and I embarrassed myself a few times that day surreptitiously following his movements while keeping my head down or pretending I was looking for something I needed just so I could position myself better for a longer appreciative stare. I found my courage after my first ten minute break (snacks could do that, I'd long learned) and pretended casual interest when I walked past his workstation pushing my empty cart back to mine.

"So have you checked out that new Marvel movie yet?" I asked, pausing beside his table. I hoped the smile I gave him didn't look too desperate. "I haven't seen it, but I usually wait till a couple of weeks after the movie comes out to go—less people in the theater bothering me that way."

Christian grinned, his eyes narrowing and sparkling and appearing even more hypnotic. "I have—me and Elliot did, actually. He got us both tickets for opening night. It's a long movie if you're planning to go." He paused and grimaced. "I always sit next to the aisle in case of restroom runs."

"How many times did you have to go? I'm asking for science."

"Twice. Not bad, then? I guess we'll have to start using the number of restroom runs as a gauge for a blockbuster movie's running time."

We both laughed at that, my gut feeling warm and squishy at that spontaneously fun, shared moment. Christian also had a way of talking to me as though I were the only person existing in the world for that sliver of time, which really drove home just how attentive and unselfish he was. By the end of our quick conversation (we talked about more than that movie for a couple of minutes), I had to go back to my workstation, stars and hearts dancing in my eyes.

It didn't take me long, but I'd already developed a massive crush on Christian yet didn't want to ruin things by asking him out. As usual, I slipped back into the background, content to just watch him and appreciate him from a safe distance. If he noticed me all but eye-fucking him, he didn't show it, and I contented myself with daydreams involving him—like dating him or even kissing him.

Was he a hugger? Did he like holding hands? I wonder what he thought about PDAs, especially between people from our tribe. He said he loved superhero movies and had a growing library of DVDs, which, apparently, Elliot borrowed from every now and then, and collected action figures. I wondered how he'd feel about things that interested me seeing as how superhero movies were fun, to be sure, but they weren't my number one entertainment love.

"D—do you like horror movies?" I asked him later. I was on my way to the break room to refill my water bottle. Again I hoped I didn't look so pathetic with the way I pretty much hung on to his every word, no matter how short our conversations tended to be.

He considered for a few seconds and shrugged. "Sure. I don't really look for them, to be honest, since I'm not a fan of slasher stuff and gore. Someone else usually pays my ticket when I actually see one in the theater. How about you?"

Always considerate of others, I thought, and I had to take note of how easy and casual he was in conversation—so much quiet confidence while I practically felt my knees knock against each other while I tamped down my usual jitteriness around him.

"I love them. Well—not the slasher stuff and gore like you, but more like creepy stuff. Ghosts and weird shit that make my hair stand."

His eyes flicked up to my hair all of a sudden, his eyes moving as though they were mapping out my—mop. Fashionable hairstyles for guys our age included the typical long layers on top and short on the sides and back. Christian's hair was straight and soft, and his bangs grazed his straight brows and drew even more attention to his eyes. Mine was wavy and thick, and Elliot's was somewhere in between the two of us, but his hair was a lighter brown where mine and Christian's were dark, dark brown.

If we were all a fairy tale, we'd be like Goldilocks's three bears, and I laughed at the thought.

"Oh? I'm game for some of that. Do you have any recommendations?"

I perked up, stunned all of a sudden. "Um—I think there's a haunted house movie coming soon. It's foreign, so there'll be subtitles..."

"I'm good with subtitles."

"Oh! Are you? Cool! I'll have to go back online to read up about it some more. All I know for now is that it's coming soon, it's from Spain, and it's creepy as hell. Um...yeah."

"Let me know, okay? No, really. I'm serious. I'd like to try other things, too. I can't live off superhero movies the rest of my life, right?" Christian laughed softly, his gaze never leaving me, and I could swear I felt the weight of his stare, and I had to swallow.

"Sure thing. Um..." Words died in my throat, and I just stood like a drop-jawed idiot in front of him because I really should have ended the conversation there, but I found that I didn't want to leave just yet and couldn't figure out how best to extend our talk. When Christian just waited for me to speak, an unexpected wave of shame swept over me, and all I could do was stammer, "Sure—I'll let you know."

And with an awkward wave—because I didn't know how to make a graceful exit—I turned and carried on with my water bottle refill, my stomach twisting from surge after surge of shame. It was a familiar feeling, and it tended to make itself felt whenever I was teetering on the precipice, about to say or do something that guaranteed my headlong tumble.

Whenever I got too excited about something, I'd run my mouth off, and my brain would just go for the ride until instinct stepped in and reined things back with a hard tug.

And that tug was always, always shame. Shame for being a complete dumbass in front of someone whose opinion I cherished. It wasn't just *looking* like a dumbass, I'd learned quickly enough. It was actively *doing* something that made me look like a miserable, attention-starved moron. I'd had crushes over the years, and I'd been lucky enough not to matter enough to them to notice me around school unless I actually talked to them.

The thing was that every time I did manage to talk to them, regardless of the subject of conversation (mostly about homework or that day's lesson), I'd always suddenly feel ashamed of myself for being so bold and thoughtless for even attempting to talk to a boy I constantly daydreamed about. He'd hear me talk and find me lacking—intelligence, charm, whatever. He'd just find me *lacking,* and I shouldn't have wasted his time with a pretty weak effort at conversation.

It was a good thing no one else was in the breakroom when I refilled my water bottle because I found myself frantically blinking away tears that were blinding me and threatening to draw unwanted attention to me once I stepped back out. I had to stick around the breakroom for a couple more minutes to gather myself, and when I returned to my workstation, Christian and Elliot were now talking and laughing at Elliot's table, and I had to duck my head and put my earbuds back on.

Chapter 12

18 May, 17—Papà's doing much, much better, and I suppose progress regarding that commission in Venice he's been talking about non-stop is helping his mood improve, which is also helping him recover. Apparently there were a few key details that needed to be sorted out between the owner and his family.

"He's a ridiculously fussy and demanding man and a fierce disciplinarian to his family," Papà said with a vague shrug as he grudgingly drank the broth Brother Rafael instructed me to make for him until he was back on his feet and bullying the chickens (we don't have chickens). "But I like working for people who know exactly what they want because it makes my job a lot easier to do. No last minute changes, no wavering over details or whatnot."

"But what if he doesn't like the way you interpreted his design?"

Papà's eyes gleamed. "Ah, Paolo, he instructed me to present him several designs, and with a lot of discussion over them, he chose his favorite and requested some changes, which I made sure he marked on the paper itself, so it's got his own handwriting there to prove he'd specifically wanted this or that, and I just followed his directions. Come now, son—you know how I work. There's no way I'm going to let a patron cheat me out of an agreement. If he complains, I'll show him that piece of paper, and he'll have to pay me extra to change things and extend my work."

"He can always tear the paper up, Papà," I countered uneasily, and he merely grunted.

"No one's ever dared attempt that," he replied. "If there's anything rich people value more than possessions, it's money. Threaten them with extra fees, and they'll balk."

The law would be on his side, he also added, and I knew it was fruitless for me to carry on an argument with him. He's determined to take on the commission, which he also insisted is going to be quite the feather in his hat. The fresco will be in a room much larger than what he's used to, and if his patron liked it, he'll commission one for another room because "vanity knows no bounds".

I continue to stay silent on my situation with Signor Amatore. I dread my lessons with Maddalena now, which is unfair to the girl, but her father's put me in a place that's growing more and more untenable by the day.

Just today, in fact, he was a touch more belligerent in his invitation to coffee and cake after the lesson, and I barely had an excuse to give him since Papà's on the mend and is up and about. If I were to say "no", he'd demand a reason, which he's already been doing, but what of tomorrow? What would he say if I told him I find his increased attention on me and not his daughter uncomfortable and unwanted?

I don't know. I don't understand anything. Why can't I just share what I love most (music) with another person without all this trouble?

*

21 May, 17—It's nice to enjoy a bit of respite from my problems. Jori was superlative today, and more than once I had to step back and shake my head, pride threatening to make my chest burst, and stop my instruction completely. The boy's taken to today's lesson so quickly and so effectively that I'm truly convinced he's a prodigy. His legato is so fluid and so smooth, I had to step in to keep the notes from melting into each other so that the harpsichord wasn't belching a string of incoherent sounds. The speed with which his fingers interpret those sixteenth notes is nothing short of astonishing.

He should have been sent to a proper music teacher—a true master, not a nearly impoverished music teacher in the country. He should be guided and shaped by someone with more talent and experience, *especially* experience, seeing as how talent can only take one so far.

I had to ask Signor Cloutier about that, and he admitted the family had considered it, but it was Jori himself who refused. The boy's not comfortable in busy spaces, and he flourishes in quieter and more spacious surroundings because those allow him to think and process at his own pace, not be pressed down on all sides with demands for his attention. I argued it would have been beneficial for the family to at least hire someone as talented and experienced as, say, Albinoni, to which Signor Cloutier merely laughed and waved away.

"M. Albinoni doesn't teach music, lad," he said. "These great men of music have better things to do with their time than show future generations how things are done. They're stewards of the arts for kings and churches, not common folk like us."

I confess I had nothing to say to that because it was all too true. Jori would more likely find a nobody like me but who perhaps equals the great men of music today in terms of talent and skill. As always, opportunity and wealth dictate the fortunes of every private music teacher, and Signor Cloutier's been quite vocal of his approval of me.

Even Gilles has been impressed with the results of my efforts, so there's that, I suppose. All the same, I can't help but mourn over lost opportunities for Jori though it also looks as though I were his own father, the way I'm constantly thinking about this boy's future prospects.

As for Maddalena, I haven't been to the Amatore house for the last couple of days as the poor girl's got a cold, and she's forced to stay in bed for now. On one hand I'm relieved because it means I don't have to face Signor Amatore for a bit of time. On the other hand, it pains me to think about that unfortunate girl being ill and believing her father truly cares for her.

Maddalena's behavior hasn't indicated a shift in that belief, and she's been blithely performing her best in front of her indifferent father. She'd see his inattention easily enough if she were to look up from the music sheet and the keyboard to find him watching me instead of her avidly—even hungrily at times, a thought that makes me shiver and not in a good way.

He knows. He knows I've become aware of his unnerving attention, which now makes me wonder if his decision to come home had anything to do with Maddalena's progress as he'd claimed. I'd like to think what I see in his eyes are nothing more than a trick played upon my senses by an uneasy mind, but I know I'll only be lying to myself.

*

25 May, 17—Maddalena's fully recovered, and I was back to pick up where we'd left off a few days ago. My poor pupil looked quite pale and wan, but her mood was high, and she all but threw herself at me for an embrace the moment I crossed the music room's threshold. The servant who used to stick around before Signor Amatore set himself up as a permanent fixture in his own home had a bit of trouble ordering the child to behave herself, but Maddalena and her newfound confidence wouldn't be dissuaded.

"I shall show my pretty tutor my happiness at seeing him again, and no one can tell me what to do!" she cried before embracing me and leaving me speechless at not only her boldness in such a display but also the frailness of her body. She felt awfully thin and light, kept earthbound surely by nothing more than the weight of her dress and all its lace and ribbons.

"Oh, signorina, that's very inappropriate!" the poor servant said, wringing her hands and casting me a very apologetic look. "Your father's going to be very upset!"

"Nonsense! He loves Signor Agnelli. He talks about him non-stop and agrees with me that he's very pretty. So angel-like."

I was speechless at the exchange, my face warming as mistress and servant argued back and forth about decorum, and before I could step in to put an end to things, the sound of a throat clearing elsewhere in the room startled us all out of our little bubble of chaos. Silence fell immediately, and I turned to find Signor Amatore half-obscured behind one of the doors to his study. He'd been there all that time, but with the double doors shut on my arrival, I'd foolishly thought he wasn't at home.

His eyes seemed to blaze when he looked at me, but I couldn't tell if it was anger or something even less desirable. He ordered the servant to leave, which she apparently was only too pleased to do, and he summoned me to his study for a brief talk before the lesson.

He also did so in front of Maddalena, which forced me to comply, and I had to leave my pupil reluctantly while urging her to get started with her scales. Thankfully she listened to me—and was soon filling the music room with her preliminary exercises.

I followed her father into his study with heavy steps and a thundering heart, and once alone with him, I watched him shut the double doors. He walked up to me with confident and easy steps, pushing me back with his increasing closeness, and I didn't realize I'd been stepping away from him until I felt my back press against a wall. He didn't even stop until he was far too close for comfort, and I know I was staring up at him with wide, panicked eyes.

He waited a moment, sure of the fact he had me cornered, and his eyes sparkled with what seemed like triumph. His mouth turned a little in a hint of a smile, his gaze heavy and bold and quite naked in their appreciation of me and perhaps even my terror of him. His gaze mapped my face, idly and brazenly, and when I thought my heart was going to be seized by its wild hammering, he finally spoke.

"I'd like to personally thank you, signore," he said in a quiet voice, that half-smile of triumph still there, "for helping my daughter find her confidence. Maddalena's growing into the kind of gentlewoman deserving of attention, and you've no small part in her improvement. She's also adamant she'd have no other teacher but you, and I quite agree, and for that reason I'd like to extend our contract for another two years.

"I understand your father's health is quite fragile, and it would be cruel to have him risk even more by taking on more demanding jobs. So as an incentive, I'd like to double your current pay, signore, if you agree to the contract extension. I won't push you, of course, but do consider Maddalena and your poor, hard-working father while you think upon it."

And that was it. He inclined his head and stepped away, turning his back on me and giving me some room and some air. I could only sag against the wall, dismayed and all the more terrified. I find I've nothing to show anyone for proof of this intimidation if I were to leave, and it would always be his word against mine in the end. I wouldn't be surprised if he were to use Maddalena as a weapon against me as well. I was so sick to my stomach after that talk that I can't even remember how our lesson turned out, but at least I wasn't pressed to stay for coffee.

Chapter 13

Mom and Dad were coming back in another two weeks, and things hadn't improved with me. If anything, my dreams seemed to have grown worse the moment they drove off. It was as if whatever was working the projector in my head decided to kill the off switch and just keep the movie going on the screen. It was a miracle I hadn't cut off any fingers or sliced my gut open by accident given how tired and woozy I felt throughout the day.

When I woke up, more often than not I'd be crying hard, curled up on myself in my bed and just sobbing miserably under my blankets. But once full consciousness took on, I couldn't remember anything save for someone's face looking sadly at me from the shadows, and that was the weirdest thing about it.

I might not remember whatever might have happened in those dreams, but that face hung on desperately in my mind.

It was a boy—a young man. Probably my age right now, and he was blond and blue-eyed, but he always, always looked at me with such grief that made my heart hurt so badly.

Something told me I knew him though I didn't recognize him one bit. I couldn't understand why I'd somehow think that, but weird shit always went on in dreams. And I didn't know why these disturbances suddenly happened, let alone why they were so intense and so problematic that they'd affect me this much during the day.

When I woke up at around four in the morning crying or completely shaken up, it would take me a while again to fall back to sleep. That would be restful as though my mind had finally vomited whatever it needed to purge from its belly, and it could actually sleep at last. But it was never enough.

And the closer it got to the end of my parents' retreat, the more convinced I got that I was in for a nice visit to the shrink. The fact that their nightly calls had gotten more and more paranoid about what I was up to—being alone, young, and newly outwardly gay surely added fuel to the Catholic fire.

"Who the hell are you?" I asked into the dark and the steadily pattering rain outside once the tears were gone, and I was again left an exhausted wreck. "I think I know you, but I can't remember anything."

* * * *

"Motherfucker!"

I froze, my gun in the middle of being reloaded with tabs, and looked up, blinking. Around me everyone was still going about their work, and I could swear Jodie screamed loud enough to bring the whole warehouse down.

"What?" I stammered, looking around. At that same moment Elliot walked by, pushing his loaded cart toward the shrinkwrap machines. "What happened? Is Jodie okay?"

"Oh. Yeah, she's fine. She just spotted a cockroach. She hates those things."

And then Elliot was gone, calm and focused as ever.

"Curtis! There's a fucking cockroach in the fucking bathroom! I have to pee!"

"Use the urinal!"

"Shut up! Where's the—fuckfuckfuckfuck!"

"We're out of bug spray! I said use the damn urinal!"

"Fuckfuckfuckfuck—oh, my fucking-ass God! It just multiplied!"

I had to laugh but took care not to be spotted by my freaked out manager. I wasn't listening to my music at the moment, so I could still hear other people talking or whistling as they worked even with the machines going on with their usual loud sounds in the background. I finished reloading my gun when someone at one of the custom framing tables suddenly whistled, and I almost dropped my gun.

I stared, unseeing, at the frames on my table waiting for me to secure them with flex-tabs.

I looked up and craned my neck to find who it was, and it was Santiago, who was framing that Poussin print when I was first interviewed for the job. He was lost in his work, his earbuds on, and he whistled along with the music he was listening to, but as before, the hair up and down my arms stood on end at hearing the song, and something told me I'd heard it before even though I didn't recognize it at all.

Maybe Ms. Garza practiced it on the organ once? I'd have to ask her, but for the time being, I needed to know.

The thing about working in a loud environment and everyone around you had earbuds or noise-canceling earphones on, getting their attention meant standing close by and waving wryly. Well, that was what I did to catch some-one's attention, anyway, and it never failed me.

Santiago smiled in that kind way of his, and he motioned for me to wait while he fumbled around with his phone.

"Sorry to bother you, but I was wondering what song it was you were whistling just now," I stammered, trying not to grimace in embarrassment.

"Oh—do you like classical music?"

Classical music? Was that what it was? I didn't know since I never listened to classical music, and my parents only listened to more vintage stuff from the sixties or even fifties sometimes. Santiago must have seen the confusion on my face because he nodded and chuckled.

"It's by Lully from his ballet *Les Bourgeois Gentilhomme*. Specifically the *Chaconne des Scaramouches, Frivelins et Arlequins*," he replied, his French sounding so pretty and fluid when he said the titles. "It's beautiful, isn't it? I can lend you my CD if you'd like to check out more."

I didn't realize I'd been holding my breath the whole time because I couldn't talk for a second or two, my voice suddenly locked, and I could only nod like an idiot.

"What else is there in the ballet?" I asked faintly once my vocal cords were finally functioning again, and that drew the biggest grin from Santiago. He raised a finger to make me hold on and detached his earbuds from his phone.

"Here. Go on, son. Check it out. Play a few tracks and see if you like them though..." he paused and laughed, his wrinkles deepening and making him look even more kindly and fatherly with his eyes twinkling along. "It looks like you already do. But go ahead and try."

My hands shook a little when I took his phone from him, and before long I was hooked up to it and listening in growing shock and horror to the tracks. One by one they played—each of them pretty short, but that did nothing to how they all affected me individually and then as a group.

Images flooded my head all of a sudden, and I didn't know where they came from.

There was a couple—maybe in their thirties, dressed in pretty rough clothes and looking as though they lived over three hundred years ago. They were talk-ing and laughing, every now and then pausing to kiss quickly, and I watched them with a burning pain in my chest, especially when the woman—the wife—turned away from her companion to look directly at me, her smile so beautiful in spite of her thinness probably from lack of good food or illness.

When she bent down to kiss my forehead, I nearly toppled over from the intense surge of pain that tore right through me.

I glanced around, but no one saw my reaction to Santiago's music. Santiago had also gone off somewhere since he wasn't at his workstation when all this happened. Christian was too busy with his work in front of me, and he had his back turned, which was a relief.

Apparently I'd started listening toward the end of the CD that had drawn my attention the first time, and Santiago's playlist moved on to a new CD, and I checked to see it was a collection of piano sonatas by someone named Scarlatti.

There was a little girl—tall for her age and awkward, slim and always looking down. I wanted to hug her for some reason. There was a little boy—a pretty ordinary kid all in all save for the fact that he looked so serious, his face a mask of complete concentration and focus as though he wanted nothing more than to master every little thing he put his mind to. I wanted to smile proudly at him because something told me he'd accomplished so much in such a short amount of time.

There were older people also emerging from some strange fog—an old man who smiled all the time, dressed finely compared to the couple, and then there was another man. Also dressed finely but much younger this time—also talking and laughing, followed by a man who was middle-aged and dignified. He was handsome enough, and there was an intensity in his eyes that made me want to leave the room he was in. Something predatory, even, but I didn't know who he was or why he was acting that way.

There were other images that came and went, and the longer I listened, the faster and more crowded the river of people and places grew in my mind until a sharp, pounding headache put an end to that.

I ripped out my earbuds and leaned against my worktable, dizzy and confused and terrified of suddenly blacking out because dark spots had begun to mess with my vision. I had to stop and pull myself together.

I didn't know how long I just stood there, gripping the edges of my worktable as though my life depended on it, and breathing rapidly. Was I having a panic attack? I never had one and didn't know what the symptoms were.

Smoothly now—smoothly. Softly. There you go. Now loudly! No, more! Forte, Andrea! Crescendo, forte!

"Adam? You okay?"

I sucked in a breath and looked up to find Curtis standing beside me, a worried Elliot next to him. Christian was away, and so were the others on the custom framing side of the warehouse. The machines had quieted down, which meant people were either on their lunch breaks or ten-minute breaks. I was still at my station, and I didn't know how long I was standing there, lost in a horrible daze and locked away in my head.

"I saw you standing there, looking all pale and—completely freaked out," Elliot said. "I tried to talk to you, but you weren't responding."

Was there any point? I wanted to go home and sleep the rest of the day away even though I knew that only meant inviting more trouble. But I was so, so tired and actually felt sick—not of the flu, though, but sick to my stomach. In the end, Curtis had to send me home early, and I couldn't argue.

Chapter 14

28 May, 17—It's my turn to be ill, which galls me as I write this, but things can't be helped. I was supposed to come with Papà to Venice, so he could show me around after he talked to his new employer (temporary, anyway) regarding this massive fresco commission.

I've been wanting to see the city. It's like a fairy tale, Papà told me, and judging from so many glowing descriptions I've heard people use when referencing Venice, I can't help but picture it as such. It must be a beautiful city, to be sure, and I'd be lying if I said I'm not crushed by this.

It was Papà who'd sent word to my pupils regarding my absence. I didn't even consider it then, but I'm glad he took care of that himself because I've a feeling Signor Amatore wouldn't have believed me.

It's so quiet here. And I feel so strange being alone in my house in the midmorning, writing in my journal, while the rest of the world carries on without me. At least the awful pain of Mamma's loss isn't so bad, and I'm able to keep myself distracted with this activity, and I've also managed (against Papà's wishes) to tidy up the house and do a bit of sweeping.

I could barely stand, and my vision swam, but I got it all done. I'd cook, too, if I could, but flagging strength and a dizzy brain are a danger in the kitchen.

Being alone and confined like this isn't a good thing to my mind right now. I keep thinking back to the recent changes in Signor Amatore toward me and especially how he doesn't seem to care that I'm aware of his inappropriate interest in me. If anything, he seemed to revel in my knowledge, and that terrifies me even more because he'll grow bolder in his efforts to subdue me.

He must have suspected my preferences for the male sex, and I don't even know if this interest in me has anything to do with my nature—like he himself is also one for men—or if this interest is just a new form of amusement to him. That is, he doesn't care whether or not I'm attracted to men or women and is merely toying with me because he can.

*

My dear Signor Agnelli,

I'm sorry to hear of your indisposition. I've inquired after you when I arrived for my lessons with our Signorina Maddalena because the girl's sulkiness betrayed the message sent to her earlier. She's quite taken with you, signore, and she's a very affection-starved child, sadly. Oh, believe me, it's nothing like an infatuation. She simply misses her "favorite pretty tutor", which made me laugh in spite of her gloom.

I decided then to write a letter to assure you Maddalena's doing quite well in your absence though if she's practicing as she should be while you're away, I didn't stick around long enough to make sure of it. Indeed, I simply can't linger there, and some subtle inquiries among the servants yielded a confirmation of a gradual change in our employer's conduct recently, coinciding with his decision to stay home more.

I shall be blunt as to be shocking to a sensible young man like you, my dear Signor Agnelli, but I've grown alarmed on your behalf, and it's got nothing to do with your illness.

Pray, signore, do *not* return to the Amatore house once you're back on your feet. I suspect you've already seen and heard enough to be ill at ease whenever you come around for Maddalena's lessons, and I boldly say that because the girl herself has casually and thoughtlessly shared her own observations of your behavior on the days leading to your illness.

You've been inexplicably distracted and nervous, she said, alternating between inattention and grating fussiness throughout her lessons. You've also been silent and distant whenever addressed by her father, which she's now wondering about, and you've stopped staying for coffee afterward.

Hearing all that from her in addition to what I've managed to glean from the servants, I'm afraid I can only come to one inevitable conclusion. One I'd hoped I wouldn't have to think about again where you're concerned—or any other newly hired, young dependent.

Yes, I'm afraid I'll have to be blunt, and seeing as how this letter is written to a friend and, indeed, one who now finds himself in the same predicament I endured before I removed myself from that house, I've no choice but to shock you and perhaps risk angering you to the point of despising me.

Our employer, Signor Agnelli, had attempted to seduce me several times in the past, which necessitated my decision to remove myself as a live-in governess to poor Maddalena. He uses his own daughter to get what he wants from someone who depends on him for survival.

Has he done that to you, too? Has he dared lay his hands on you? Has he attempted rape? He's done all of those to me, and I had no one to turn to for help, being alone—an orphan—with no real prospects in the world. You at least still have your father though I understand if it galls you to confide the truth in him. Had I still parents, I'd have kept my troubles to myself, too.

Signor Amatore's sudden concern for his daughter's improvement, which prompted his decision to spend half the day at home, is a sham. I've seen similar theatrics from him when I still lived with the family, and he loathes his own flesh and blood because she's a reminder of his entrapment, having been forced to marry the girl's mother after getting her with child.

It was his misfortune he'd tampered with the daughter of a very influential man who'd have easily ruined him if he were to refuse to fix his mistake, you see. And here we are now.

He will tempt you with honeyed promises. He will ingratiate himself or perhaps use his position to intimidate you into accepting his one-sided terms. In my case, he offered to extend my contract with him while doubling my pay, which is an insult in the worst way.

Am I a prostitute to him? Are you? I flatly refused, of course, and intend to make good my present contract, which ends in a fortnight. Unfortunately poor Maddalena will suffer the most from this, for I've no intention of returning, and I'm afraid the girl will be bound for the convent if no one applies for the vacancy.

And there it is—the truth all laid out in all its ugliness, signore. Forgive me for perhaps ruining things for you, but I daresay Signor Amatore alone has managed that already. All I've done with this letter is provide you with ghastly context, and if you don't act now, you'll surely be ruined.

Oh, he won't be blamed at all, you know. I know how men of his stature spin and embellish the truth to their advantage. They'll emerge the victims in such a sordid drama, the real victims of their vile appetites blamed for the stain on their reputation and character.

You, my dear Signor Agnelli, will do well to save yourself now. Maddalena herself will be a victim in the end given her father's degrading use of her as bait, and I grieve to say perhaps she's better off sheltered in a convent, where she's at least beyond her father's sickening grasp.

She can pursue her studies in peace there and be surrounded by women who have her best interests at heart. And she'll be under the Virgin's protection, too, which the poor child deserves more than anything since in spite of her wealth and privilege, she's still very much alone and dangerously exposed.

Do take care, signore. I will pray for you and your father.

With deepest respect,
Ines Tessaro

*

28 May, 17—(continued) I'm absolutely terrified of going back to the Amatore house. I thought at first Signora Tessaro was being shockingly spiteful because of some problem she might have had with Signor Amatore, but what would she gain from lying? I could have easily put the blame on her for being embittered over rejection or disappointments, having played that game to our employer—the very same one she accuses him of.

But I've already been harassed. I continue to be harassed and intimidated by a man I thought had his daughter's best interests at heart. He even treated me like a common prostitute, as Signora Tessaro called it, with his generous offers and implied demands. Implied, yes, because he didn't have to outright tell me he wanted me in his bed.

All I need to do is think back on his behavior and the awful weight of his hungry gaze whenever we're in the same room. And now that I have her story as well, I'm even more horrified at the recent pay raise I was given before he came forward with his honeyed offer.

Signora Tessaro speaks the truth, and she gains nothing by exposing herself to me in a brutally frank letter. I've heard her talk fondly, even lovingly, of Maddalena, and I know we share the same concern for that girl's well-being.

By refusing to accept an extension of her employment, she's giving up a connection that's already grown dear to her in the span of only a year, but what else can she do? I understand where she's coming from though for both of us, the solution to our problem means abandoning our charge to her father's whims.

The more I think upon it, though, the more I find myself agreeing to her conviction that poor Maddalena will be better off in the convent if things do go down that road. My poor girl! To have her life ruined—and the trust poorer dependents ought to have in their betters compromised, perhaps irreversibly—by the selfish turns of a man so used to his power and wealth!

And worse yet, how can I make my decision known to Papà? I know I don't want to carry on tutoring Maddalena, but what will I tell him, especially since we're already benefiting from my recent raise? Will my own father think me capable of doing something so vile as to exchange favors for it?

No, no, I won't think it. Papà's better than that. He deserves the truth, and I can't lie to him, but I'm back to being quite stuck on how best to broach the subject.

I'm still feeling quite ill—in fact even more so after reading Signora Tessaro's letter. I only hope Signor Amatore won't be sending someone around to find out if my illness is a cheap pretense to stay away. And Jori's also deprived of his lessons, but at least with him I can be assured of his continued practice in my absence. His grandfather and brother will make sure of it.

Poor Maddalena—I really do hope for the best for that unfortunate girl. I can hear Papà downstairs, and I nearly vomited on my journal just hearing his voice calling for me. God help me. I still don't know what to tell him, and I'm starting to panic.

The Virgin will guide me, I know. It's hard to let go and put my faith in her with my mind in such a muddle, but Mamma would insist that I trust her in this, and Mamma was never wrong.

Chapter 15

The blond boy had a mark around his neck—something like a bruise but was also a mark the shape of a line across his throat. In my dream he just stood there and looked at me, anguish in his reddened eyes. For a moment nothing happened, but then he spoke, the slight change in his air making me think he was just waiting for me to pay full attention to him.

"I wanted to follow you," he said softly, and to my shock, he spoke in Italian, which I understood perfectly. "Why did you have to leave?"

Church bells rang and drew me gradually out of my dream. It was a change from suddenly jolting awake from a natural fight-or-flight response when it came to these dreams. I actually felt reluctance to waking up this time, and I blinked my eyes open to a dark living room. It took me a moment to remember how I got there and why the hour was so late when it felt as though I'd only stumbled across the threshold and crumpled onto the sofa.

The rain had returned, the usual heavy pounding now a lighter but steady drumming that never failed to soothe my nerves. I glanced at my watch, squinting in the dim light to find the time to be almost six. I'd been sleeping for five hours, and I realized I actually felt regenerated.

The bells continued, tolling the hour and the reminder of my family's—and likely other devout Catholic families'—ritual of praying the Angelus before dinner.

Mom used to lecture me before about the old ways of this devotion, but modern times made it pretty much impossible to do it the old-fashioned three times daily thing. Mom and Dad were also at work most of the day while I was at school and then at work afterward.

It meant this practice grew more and more infrequent and practiced only when we had the time and when we were all together at home. Once I started my senior year in high school, it was only Mom who prayed regularly though Dad joined her every now and then, depending on when he arrived home.

I had the excuse of homework and after-school activities, and I didn't at all feel badly about it.

This time, though, I wondered if going to San Tadeo church would help me—not necessarily for prayers but just for some quiet meditation. I'd never gone to that old mission church whenever the Angelus bell rang, but I figured it should be open for early evening devotions if it was kept open throughout the day for half the week, at least. I was sure Mom would approve if she found out, but I wouldn't hear the end of her praises.

I was soon dressed in my warmest clothes and walking out into the fog, the rain having stopped again and given way to a thick and moody aerosol blanket. People walked in and out of the fog, looking more like specters than corporeal figures.

Street, store, and house lights formed fuzzy pockets of illumination, and the air smelled heavily of rain. We were in for another deluge soon enough, and I tucked my umbrella under my arm as I made my way to San Tadeo.

The bells had long stopped their ringing, and I arrived at the church to find the doors shut but unlocked when I tested them. The old chandeliers weren't on, but the wall sconces were, and a few votive candles also burned in their holders. No one was inside the church when I entered, my footsteps echoing a little in the empty space. I looked around me, frowning a little the deeper I walked into the silent, gloomy old church.

There was something in the air that didn't feel familiar and yet it did. Had there been upgrades done lately? I couldn't see it if that were so since everything appeared pretty normally, every detail about San Tadeo painstakingly replicated based on photographic archives of the original mission church before it burned down.

There had always been a heavy air of stagnation in the church itself, and praying inside felt as though one were caught in a state of suspension, with time captured and held static forever.

As I walked down the center aisle toward the altar, the feeling grew into a weird mix of old and new, past and present, and I couldn't stop looking around me to find whatever it was that had triggered the feeling. Unless it was nothing more than an effect of the freak weather system, my ongoing sleep troubles, and the time of the day—I just felt a touch off.

I genuflected and then sat down before the altar, gazing at the old, old and intricately decorated reredos, allowing my mind to open and clean itself of unwanted thoughts that usually cluttered it. Eventually I felt relaxed enough to close my eyes and pray in my own way—sitting down and not kneeling like I usually did. Not the Angelus, no, but a plea for guidance and strength in my own awkward and stumbling way.

Luckily enough, I didn't get assaulted by memories of my dreams and recent incidents at work, but that feeling of being off continued throughout my meditation. I was relaxed but not to the point where I felt comfortable being alone in that silent and static place.

Sometime during this, the soft but distinct creaking of the front door gently broke the stillness of the church. I didn't hear footsteps, but it didn't matter. There was some comfort to be had in finally being in the company of one more person though it didn't seem to make much of a difference to my odd, off-center feeling that kept a fuller state of peace just beyond reach.

"*Ave Maria, gratia plena, Dominus tecum...*"

I sighed and couldn't help a small smile. There was something about prayers spoken in Latin that exalted them in my mind.

"*Benedita tu in mulieribus, et beneditus fructus ventris tui, Iesus. Sancta Maria, Mater Dei, ora pro nobis peccatoribus, nunc, et in hora mortis nostrae. Amen.*"

A quick pause followed, during which I pegged the devotee to be male though he whispered his prayer, the silence of the church carrying the words in spite of the very private manner of its recitation.

There was also a fervency in the way the prayer was spoken, a strong emotion propelling it, even, though I couldn't figure out what. The prayer started again, the words a little less fluid and peppered with clumsy pauses every now and then. I frowned as I kept my eyes closed, this time straining my ears now that my concentration had been broken by the newcomer.

"*Why me? I haven't done anything wrong. Why me?*"

My eyes flew open, and I shot to my feet, spinning around and finding myself alone in the church. My hair stood on end, my heart beat a frantic rhythm, and my breaths were a little ragged as I searched the empty pews for signs of someone else having just been there.

The church doors were shut as they'd always been, but I could have sworn I heard them creak open and close—softly, sure, but the hollow silence allowed the smallest sound to carry, and I was fully alert and pretty hyper-aware of my surroundings after clearing my head of the usual clutter.

No, there wasn't another person there with me even though I distinctly heard the whispered prayer. I heard the emotion behind it. The despair and the painful grief. I wasn't dreaming this time, and that made my unease grow even more, slowly turning into terror the longer I stuck around the church. I got out of the pew, gave the altar a final, distracted gesture of respect by genuflecting again, and walked down the center aisle.

My skin prickled the entire time, and I could swear the hair on my head was steadily rising.

"Why am I made like this? Please, are you testing me? Please make me whole and normal!"

My strides quickened, and by this time I stopped looking around me, my gaze resolutely fixed on the doors leading to freedom. I was going insane, I kept thinking, but the more I told myself that, the less convinced I grew in spite of all signs to the contrary.

I was hearing voices now, even while I was alert and conscious of everything around me. I was feeling off-balance without understanding why and how, and what terrified me even more was the realization that those voices—there were two, I found—prayed in German and then French, and I understood every word somehow even though I never learned either language.

I reached the front doors and were about to throw them open when movement off to my side sent me yelping and staggering against the doors with a dull thump. I was staring now at the side chapel, where a man had just emerged and stopped at the entrance, regarding me in some surprise.

He looked ordinary enough, dressed plainly and even a little raggedly, his careworn features indicating years of hard work and suffering endured in silence. But there was nothing threatening or frightening about him as he observed me cautiously from the safety of the side chapel's entrance.

"Are you all right?" he finally asked in a slightly tremulous and rough voice as though he hadn't spoken in years. He also spoke with a heavy accent though his English was fluent. "I thought I heard you running."

I nodded after taking a deep, calming breath, and even managed a faint smile of relief. What a feeling to have someone there with me. I knew now I wasn't imagining things when I heard the church doors open, but I had no answer to the voices.

"I'm fine, thanks," I replied. "I thought I heard something that freaked me out a little, but—it looks like I was wrong. Thank you for asking, though."

The man nodded, still looking a little cautious, and I didn't blame him. "Good. That's good. Well—have a good evening, then. And you know the church will be open to you whenever you need it."

I thanked him again and opened half of the double doors, my focus on him just as he kept his gaze on me the whole time—thoughtful, questioning, and even wondering, I thought, which was a curious thing to say about a stranger's state of mind after a handful of seconds' worth of awkward conversation. But there was something like wonder in the way he looked at me—as though he couldn't quite believe I was there or I was actually talking to him.

The fog seemed to have thickened even more while I was inside the church, and all but hugging my umbrella against me, I hurried down the stone steps and didn't stop my relentless pace till I was back home.

A thought—a startling realization—had hounded me throughout my walk, and I tried not to entertain it, but once swaddled in more familiar and comfortable surroundings, warmth and light chasing away my frayed nerves, that thought took hold and refused to be ignored. It had something to do with the church doors, I found. While I was in the church, I heard them creak, but they made no sound when I opened them to leave.

Ms. Garza's throwaway comments in the past regarding the strict maintenance schedule of San Tadeo included the near-obsessive oiling of old hinges, especially the entrance doors. They used to creak loudly, and that'd become such an annoying distraction to worshippers that their maintenance had gone over the top.

Chapter 16

30 May, 17—I continue to be ill though I thought I had a breakthrough yesterday. Papà's beside himself with worry even if he shows nothing but indulgence and good humor around me. The longer I remain sick, too, the more anxious he gets about fresco-work, but at least he's quite settled with that palazzo commission. That is, he and his new employer have agreed upon terms at last, and Papà's set to begin work next week.

The arrangements where we're concerned, however, isn't satisfactory for both of us, but needs must, and this new job of his will be the highest-paying commission he'll have. There's also the benefit of having his name and his excellent work spread among Signor Di Pasqua's peers, which is, I admit, a very exciting prospect.

So Papà will spend half of each day there and will either remain for the night or travel back home, depending on how he feels. I've reassured him I can take care of myself if he weren't around.

From what I understand, he's allowed to hire a couple of temporary help, and he's got connections for that, so there's really no need for me to fret on his account. I expect to keep a close eye on his health, however. If there's anything Signor Amatore said that's painfully hit the mark, it would be Papà's age and growing fragility.

And speaking of Signor Amatore, I've had a servant of his deliver a gift of chocolates to me yesterday with a curt note simply expressing good wishes for my speedy recovery. And for what, I wondered? So he could harass me all over again once I'm back to teach his daughter? I keep thinking of Maddalena and what sort of trouble's now slowly forming in her future—unless a generous and kind relation would take her in, of course, a prospect that didn't even cross my mind till I received that box of chocolates (which I gave to Papà, who has a terrible sweet tooth).

Yes, I do hope someone would step in to help my unfortunate girl should things spiral out of control.

I don't know whether or not Signora Tessaro's shocking note is to blame for my current unease, but I've been restless and suddenly fearful of something I don't even understand, let alone identify.

I'm afraid of showing my face again at the Amatore house, of course, but this new unsettling feeling is very different. It's low, insistent, and steady. I keep feeling dread—a foreboding—without knowing why. It's all in my head, I'm sure. Perhaps a nap will help even if I've been napping on and off all day, every day, which is really starting to fray my nerves and sour my temper.

*

2 June, 17—To be a child again! Jori and Maddalena were beside themselves with joy at my return, which I flatter myself to think had everything to do with my company (and my position as their music teacher, of course). And what a welcome back I enjoyed from my pupils—near-perfect performances!

Signor Cloutier laughed and welcomed me back with a hearty shake of the hand as well as a generous spread of French bakes with tea before *and* after Jori's lessons. Jori himself stuck around and enjoyed the repast with us, and while he was still the quiet and solemn boy I've grown to admire and adore, he clearly loved every spirited minute spent in his overly chatty grandfather.

Gilles was expected to return tomorrow from another trip to France, but it appears that Signor Cloutier's been doing a tremendous job keeping Jori entertained and distracted from his brother's absence.

My ongoing discussion with Papà regarding his Venetian commission and my work here so far has yielded somewhat satisfying results. Given his health, he was obliged to agree to simply staying in Venice all week while I keep my schedule—at least with Jori as well as possible new pupils to teach. With Papà away, I expect to have more time to take in two more pupils since my hours won't be so structured around his schedule.

I went to the Amatore house with my heart in my throat, but as it turned out, there was no need for me to fret because Signor Amatore was away—has been away since the second day of my illness, in fact, and I've been gone for four days altogether.

Maddalena, poor thing, nearly exploded in a wild fit of childish excitement at seeing me again, even bursting into tears when she threw herself at me for a tight and desperate embrace. Decorum again suffering this time, much to her servant's dismay, who was back to wringing her hands and chastising her mistress to no avail.

My heart broke when I soothed Maddalena because I knew too well our time together will be coming to an end soon. I've yet to broach the subject to Papà, and I refuse to say a word about it for now to my unfortunate pupil. And I do agree with her father, at least, where her improvements are concerned.

Maddalena might still be too tall and too thin for her age, but she carries herself with much greater confidence now, easily keeping her chin up and her gaze straight and bold. She's more expressive and talkative than ever, and I've yet to hear her complain of imperfections. She's also quite taken with Scarlatti's work, claiming her father has had a group of friends come by for dinner a couple of days ago, and one of them played Scarlatti on the harpsichord. Maddalena had listened, enraptured.

I asked her where her father was and how long he was expected to stay away. She shrugged, testing the keyboard and depressing keys at random.

"He just went away with his friends," she said. "When they come around, he always goes with them when they leave, and I think they spend time at someone's villa somewhere. I don't know when he'll be back, but he was quite put out when you were sick, Signor Agnelli. He was like a wild animal caged, pacing and growling and muttering to himself. I was heartily glad his friends came by to take him away. I don't like it when he's in one of those moods."

And how many times has he indulged in this surliness?

"Right before Signora Tessaro packed up and left her room," Maddalena replied with conviction that turned my blood cold. "But I'm glad she's still teaching me. I really like her though I do miss her sometimes. It's awfully lonely here with her now living elsewhere."

Then she proceeded to impress me with her scales followed by a movement from one of our unknown talents who's been working hard against the tide to reach the heights easily scaled by Scarlatti and his ilk—a Signor Uccello. A man whose works I've taken the trouble to purchase with my own savings whenever I can so my pupils can benefit from excellent (thought obscure and uncelebrated) talent.

I don't know when her father will return, but I'll take all the respite I can get before he darkens my steps again. It's a terribly ungrateful thing to say about one's employers, to be sure, but he's forced me into this, and I know things will never be the same again.

*

5 June, 17—Gilles was quite pleased at hearing about Papà's newest commission, saying he knows Signor Di Pasqua. Apparently the gentleman's an absurdly rich connoisseur of art, music, and literature, and he's purchased a few beautiful pieces of furniture (gaming table and chairs, bombe commodes, and others) from the Cloutier family's business.

And he also has a ward who might be interested in music lessons, Gilles appended with an encouraging smile, and my mood perked up. For a while now, I've been fretting over how best to mitigate the damage my exit from teaching Maddalena will likely cause, and perhaps with some excellent references, I might be able to take on this ward of Signor Di Pasqua's.

It would be very good, of course, to be able to work closely with Papà, and perhaps we can make such an arrangement so that I can spend a portion of the week in Venice and the rest of the days here, so I can continue working with Jori. Travel expenses might be awful in the end, but it's worth considering and discussing with Papà.

Gilles had gone on and, like an old gossip though he might be too young, said Signor Di Pasqua is extremely exacting, demanding, and strict where his family's concerned. His ward is an orphan and a grand nephew, so to speak, and if I were to be hired as a private music tutor for him, the lad would be my oldest pupil to date at eighteen.

I expect these music lessons—should I be hired for them—will be nothing more than a hobby for someone who has everything and is quite likely bored to tears with wealth and is simply looking for another faddish distraction.

*

My dearest Signor Agnelli,

Pray do *not* come to the Amatore house at all. I'm writing you quickly and am hoping my letter is halfway coherent as I can't keep my hand from shaking so much. Maddalena's been whisked away, and I've yet to find out where she was taken, but she's not at home at the moment, and the servants are all in a great panic.

Signor Amatore's dead. He arrived late last night without his friends, went about his evening as always, but this morning the house was invaded by a man half-mad with grief, claiming Signor Amatore has murdered his poor daughter. I've yet to learn more about this, but it all happened while I was in the library with Maddalena.

There was a great deal of shouting, furniture being thrown around, and glass breaking. The library's situated far enough for us not to hear anything else but the most severe noise like what I've described. Then servants came running and crying out for their master. I do believe the door to the study was locked throughout the fracas.

But the long and short of it, signore, is our employer's dead—stabbed several times by a distraught man who's been dragged away while screaming his daughter's name.

What I've managed to gather from frantic servants who heard most of the exchange was that Signor Amatore had gotten a fourteen-year-old girl with child—likely raped—and the unhappy girl hanged herself even after her parents had reassured her she wasn't going to be thrown out in the streets. The father, already driven nearly insane by grief, also pushed his way into the house quite drunk, and now here we all are.

I've yet to confirm these scattered and delirious reports, all of which were told to me in a frenzied panic. Dear heaven, I can't stop thinking about poor Maddalena. She might be at a friend's house right now, but I can't seem to get a proper answer regarding her true whereabouts.

I can't write any more. Rest assured, signore, I'll write you again unless you prefer to speak with me in person. My address is on the back of this sheet for you.

Yours,
Ines Tessaro

Chapter 17

I spent a lot of time looking up classical music from the time of Lully, my searches coming up with way too many composers for me to follow through realistically. But those whose music worked like a blow to my head became my focus after a while, and I used my savings to buy streaming music for my phone.

Considering how many compositions each had to their name, I had to randomly pick collections—at least money was a major deciding factor in this case, which meant sticking to cheaper collections even though they weren't comprehensive enough.

Santiago was a massive fan of Baroque music, and I listened to a pretty wide range from his playlist. The ones that stuck to me the most and the longest were the composers he said (when I asked him) were from the early Baroque period, specifically those born in the 17th century and died sometime in the mid-18th century. Italian composers and a couple of French composers ended up having their work downloaded into my phone.

With the weather still being pretty weird and wild outside, the music turned into the perfect accompaniment to it, and I puttered around the house with my earbuds on, taking care of chores to Scarlatti's piano sonatas, reading to Couperin, resting up and eventually napping to even earlier music: Palestrina.

Throughout the time spent immersing myself in these compositions, my previous panic and anxiety gradually and gently melted away. Comfort and ease took their place, and I surprised myself when I realized the comfort came from a deeper place—familiarity laced with deep, unswerving affection.

Somehow I knew this music though I grew up hardly listening to classical music, if at all, and what would have been a massive shock from this kind of revelation never really happened.

If anything, I suppose opening myself to the strangeness of that idea and not only accepting such a bizarre thought while exploring new musical territory helped me reach that place of peace. Maybe sometimes simply accepting something without a struggle was all I needed.

Maybe that was the only way for me to sort out my sleep troubles, especially when they were slowly forging a connection with my waking hours and these memories I knew were never part of my past. Or my past as I was now.

I'd heard of past lives so many times before, largely in fiction or videos or even movies or TV shows though I understood certain cultures also had the idea of reincarnation woven into their beliefs. So many people had a bunch of different thoughts on how that worked or if was even true. Well, I suppose if something's nothing more than an unproven idea, people can interpret it however way they wanted.

And if there were such a thing as a past life, what would be mine? I couldn't even manage a hazy glimpse with all the scattered pieces I kept collecting from dreams and music and disembodied voices. But I was slowly embracing them now, and that was a start.

The low light, the heater warming the house, a full stomach, the steady patter of rain, and soft piano music in my ears—all of them together made for a potent combo, and I was down for the count with piano sonatas lulling me easily into a midday nap. And this time around, I wasn't afraid of it though I nervously wondered what kind of dream waited for me.

* * * *

He was sulking again, and I was so close to tearing my hair out. I didn't want to encourage him, though, by succumbing to his pouts and childish complaints because I wasn't being paid to do that. His granduncle would be furious, though, and while he wouldn't take his anger out on Andrea in physical form, my pupil would be shut up again for a day or maybe two without a plate of food.

"Andrea, please—we don't have much time together. Please show me how well you understand arpeggios," I begged. I dared not come any closer when he was in a mood because he'd press his advantage over me once I displayed a hint of weakness. And God knew, I had too many of them where he was concerned.

He glared at me, his cheeks flushed. "Scarlatti's an ass. What, did he expect people to come out of their mothers' wombs already dexterous on the harpsichord? Just look at this monstrosity! Who does this shit?"

I glanced uneasily at the double doors of the music room, which had been slammed shut by a furious signore. I didn't know if he listened for music coming from this room whenever I was there for Andrea, and my pupil's passionate insults—while they normally roused my temper—now fell short. I'd lent him

my precious and only copy of Scarlatti's exercises, which were gifted to me by
my own music teacher (who died actually believing I was born to play for kings,
but he was mentally failing by then), and he fought tooth and nail against each
lesson.

"Here," I said at last, striding across the space and waving Andrea off the
bench. "Let me show you."

He stood up and placed himself to the side of the elaborate instrument, all
the while glowering at me while I took his place at the keyboard. I tried to ignore the resentful heat of his stares and positioned my hands, and in another
second, the music room was filled with the Sonata in D, which Andrea constantly massacred that day. I couldn't tell if he were doing so on purpose to
frustrate me or if he actually didn't understand the exercise. It was a favorite of
mine—a gentler piece in spite of its complexity, the music a playful yet somehow relaxed-sounding one to me.

When I was still a child learning through the generosity and kindness of my
tutor and his wife, I couldn't be made to stop playing this piece and move on to
a new exercise.

My thoughts immediately drifted back to those days all those years ago,
when Signor Belluomo eagerly took me in at a ridiculously reduced rate because he deeply, sincerely believed I was meant for great things with my natural
gifts. My eyes stung at the memories though my hands didn't falter once. I loved
that old man and his wife as I would my own grandparents, my knowledge of
music as well as this special collection of harpsichord exercises, which Signor
Belluomo even signed a dedication to me prior to his death, being his ultimate
gift to me.

I could only hope I continued to give him reasons to be proud of me even
if I didn't play for royal audiences.

"There," I said once I finished the piece, waving a hand at the keyboard.
"Start slow if you wish and progress—"

I couldn't finish my sentence. How could I, when Andrea's lips were suddenly on mine, and I was too distracted by the exercise to notice just how quickly and quietly he'd moved and closed the distance between us. He'd bent close
to kiss me—his second kiss since we started our lessons and the second kiss I'd
tried to avoid after he'd done the same thing just a week ago.

"I'm trying to start slow," he whispered against my mouth before kissing me again. "But I'm afraid you'll be gone by the time I achieve the proper speed."

* * * *

My parents' landline ringing woke me up, and I realized the music had already stopped. I pulled the earbuds out, yawning, and set my phone down on the coffee table. The house was nice and comfortably warm, the steady rhythm of the rain outside doing a pretty good job of tempting me to let the call go to the answering machine.

My parents didn't care much—or trust—the newest bling in technology and kept their own phones as a grudging admission those things were practical in the case of emergencies. A landline couldn't be hacked, they'd argued, and here we were. At least it forced me to get up and walk to the sideboard Grandma left us.

"Hello? Mom? Is everything okay?"

There was a short pause before the voice replied. "Hello? Uh—Adam? Hey, it's Christian from work. I got your number from Curtis after Elliot told me about what happened yesterday."

It took me an embarrassing moment to realize who was talking to me then, and if I could burn my hair off my scalp from the heat now suffusing my face, I'd have done it without a hitch. "Christian?" I stammered. "Oh, hey—I'm sorry, I didn't recognize your voice. I—I'm good, thanks. I just needed an extra day off to rest."

"You called out, yeah. Anyway, I'm glad you're good. I'll tell Elliot. He was a little freaked yesterday and bugged me to check up on you."

I had to smile at that. "Tell him thank you, and I'll be back tomorrow."

"Cool. Hey, are you free tomorrow night? There's a B-horror movie I want to check out at the discount theater. It'll be great if you could come, but no pressure. If you'd rather stay home and rest, that's fine, too."

Christian was asking me out? I blinked, held the phone away so I could stare at it in confusion, and then press it against my ear again. I must have looked like someone in a sitcom right then, but I was too stunned to even be embarrassed by my reaction to Christian's invitation.

"Um—yeah, I'm free. What time did you want to meet? You don't have to pick me up, by the way. The theater's just a five-minute walk from my house. It'll be a hassle for you to have to double back for such a short distance."

"Oh, is it? Okay, how about eight? Maybe we can hang out at an all-night pizza parlor after, but we can talk about it then. Is that all right with you? Sorry, this is sort of a spur-of-the-moment thing. I just happened to drive past the the-ater and saw what was on. Then it was all online searches and stuff—you know how it is," Christian said, his words coming out in a babbling stream that drew a quiet chuckle out of me.

Was he nervous? God, if anyone had a right to be nervous being asked out on a date with Christian, it'd be me.

A few more details were hashed out, and then the call ended, and I was standing and staring in shock and confusion at the phone I'd just returned to its cradle. Christian had just asked me out, I thought, my brain still unable to wrap itself around the idea. Where the hell did that come from?

Was he actually interested in me that whole time?

I was so taken aback I didn't realize I was marching into the kitchen for something to eat and calm my nerves until I had a spread on the table. Then I burst out laughing—giddy, excited, awestruck. I'd been on a couple of dates with guys in the past, but nothing came from them. I was too tightly wound up to let anyone go past dinner out, and those had been planned carefully ahead of time.

Christian's call came way out of left field, and judging from the mild awk-wardness of our conversation, I could tell he was working things out as we went along. As if he'd never planned to call me and ask me out on a date, but he'd been made to do it—why? Worry over my well-being? Elliot was a sweet guy, and it didn't surprise me at all that he'd get Christian to check up on me. I should thank Elliot for being the catalyst, it looked like—maybe buy him lunch.

Chapter 18

7 June, 17—The Amatore house is still locked up, and I've asked around and discovered everyone's left. Someone said the servants were all released, but as for Maddalena, no one knows. The poor girl must be at a relation's house now, far from here and beyond my reach. Surely it's the best thing anyone can do for her now that she's an orphan.

I continue not to know or fully understand the particulars, but it appears what Signora Tessaro said in her letter is true. My deceased employer was known to wander in more ways than one, motivated probably by beauty and power—beauty in the person he'd chosen for his hunt and power (his) over this person.

If Signora Tessaro, this unhappy girl whom he'd raped, and I are any indication, Signor Amatore used his position of power to intimidate his chosen victim. Gender had no bearing on his choices, I believe, since he came after both, and the only thing linking us was our poverty and, in my case and Signora Tessaro's, our dependence on him.

I know nothing about this dead girl other than she was a cobbler's youngest daughter and that she'd been raped. Her family also lived twenty miles away, and her father had followed her seducer here to avenge her. Was Signor Amatore known to have bullied and persecuted helpless people to bed? I don't want to think so, but I'm afraid I can't help but expect a string of new accusations to come to light.

I dread to think about the victims—their number—and how this man managed to get away with his crimes for heaven knows how long. I reckon his position and connections protected him until now.

Maddalena had said her father went away with his friends quite regularly, and they'd be gone for days with the poor child ignorant of her parent's whereabouts. For all we know, he'd been seducing his way up and down Italy and leaving a horde of bastards in his wake while his daughter was abandoned to her lonely existence.

I don't want to think so badly of anyone, and I ought to pray to the Virgin for forgiveness, but I can't help it. Not after what I've been through and what Signora Tessaro had endured.

Would I now be tainted by association with so many dreadful things coming to light after this awful business? I hope not. I hope my efforts at finding new pupils to teach won't be jeopardized by this tragedy.

The cobbler's fate—I'd sooner not think upon it. This is all too terrible to lose myself in. I can only pray for his soul and the soul of his daughter. What a wretched chain of events! Now two families are without their fathers, their names forever linked to this murder, their prospects uncertain. I hope not. I truly hope something good will someday come out of this, and everyone can move on.

Papà's been shaken up badly after learning about it, but nothing compares to the look of heartbreak on his face when I finally told him about my experiences and Signora Tessaro's. I hope I didn't overstep when I shared the lady's ordeal. He pulled me close for a long and tight embrace, murmuring apologies he didn't need to make for pressing me to accept Signor Amatore's generous offer of employment after my interview.

"I placed you in harm's way," he said brokenly while fighting back his tears and holding my face in his hands. "I pushed you to apply for the post and take it. I didn't know, Paolo. I didn't know. I don't understand how predators can hide so well."

I reassured him over and over again there was simply no way for him to know about Signor Amatore's true nature and his vices. He was a widower with one child, he was constantly away on business, and he was filthy rich. That had been all we knew of him, and Papà was right about predators.

They're everywhere, aren't they? They look and act no differently from everyone else, which allows them to cast their nets at unsuspecting victims, who're doomed to remain ignorant about the danger until it's too late.

How can I now reassure myself that my next employer is a good person? I've been awfully lucky with Signor Cloutier. After this sordid business, how fairly will I be able to judge my employer's character? No, I shouldn't think that, or I'll never find work. I'll pray again, and perhaps this time around, the Virgin will also guide me.

*

12 June, 17—Papà's gone off to Venice for a few days to finalize his hiring of temporary assistants. So far I haven't been so fortunate in my search for new music posts to apply for given how rare such positions are nowadays—especially in such a town so removed from the busier and larger cities.

Surely I won't be hitting one wall after another had we lived in places like Padova, but such is my luck, and I'm now seriously contemplating giving up and seeking any random position to supplement my income from tutoring Jori.

I suppose I can always find work at a shop if there were any that sold anything to do with music. I confess I've never tried selling anything in the past since all of my time and energy had been fixed on my lessons and my efforts in continuing Signor Belluomo's desire to see Italian music flourish among the younger generations.

I happen to love and enjoy teaching music, too, which has tempered any disappointments regarding any expectations for royal appointments or simply performing before kings and queens.

Surely there are music shops around here.

(continued) I've just been out for a fairly exhaustive search, and my efforts are disappointing. This isn't a major city with a rich culture, and I can only find artisans, and even then, they aren't looking for extra help. I'll continue searching, of course, but this can only mean even stricter economy with my greatly reduced income.

Papà hasn't said anything about my future, but I can see the concern in his eyes and the sadness with which he's been observing me when he thinks I'm not looking or observing him back.

I know his heart's broken for me. I know it isn't fair with luck having a heavier hand than hard work in shaping my future. But I really do try as hard as I can to surpass everyone's expectations. That's all I can do, isn't it? Try hard and work even harder.

*

16 June, 17—I had the good fortune of running into Signora Tessaro while out and about, responding to a couple of inquiries pertaining to music-teaching posts. She looked quite pale and drawn, worry etched in her otherwise pretty features, and it was she who invited me to her favorite coffee shop for a conversation.

"Our Maddalena's been sent to the convent," she said following an uneasy pause after we sat down. "I don't know where exactly, but it's far from here. Somewhere closer to Rome, I suspect."

"What about her family? Don't they want her?"

It had been in her father's will, apparently, that she'd be sent to the convent for study and prayer but not necessarily with a future as a nun. She's too young at the moment and simply needed the more sedate and stripped down environment a convent can provide.

How ironic was it that her rake of a father would plan such a thing for his unwanted daughter? No, come to think of it, I suppose it isn't ironic at all. A convent's a very convenient place to send a burden, isn't it? A generous payment to the abbess for the girl's education and maintenance as well as support for the convent, and all will be well.

I grieve for Maddalena still, but I do find some comfort in the thought that at least she'll have these ladies of God around her all day, every day. They'll protect and guide her, and with any luck, she'll emerge from this a strong and intelligent gentlewoman free of her father's stain.

As for Signora Tessaro, she's doing well enough in spite of her limited prospects.

"I've been hired for a new post as a governess," she said with a tired smile. "It'll take me a good distance from here, I'm afraid, but I can write you all the same if you wish to be distracted by my inane babbling. Believe me, signore, being a governess isn't very exciting, and I'll likely entertain you with a litany of woes instead."

I had to laugh. "It's something I can relate to, I expect, but my case is a great deal more limited in scope, so you have me at a disadvantage."

"I'd rather have your disadvantage, young man," she replied, chuckling.

My heart sank at the thought, however, in spite of my happiness on her account. It was good she was able to find a new post—one somewhere in France, in fact, thanks to a few connections she's managed to make throughout her still-short time as a governess, and she's incredibly fortunate there.

She told me before we parted not to give up, that I'm too talented and too hard a worker to languish in failure. She even reassured me my future's much brighter than I think, and we parted with bittersweet goodbyes and well-wishes. I did make sure to let her know I'm only too happy to be distracted with her accounts of teaching spoiled, young children, so her letters will be most welcome.

*

19 June, 17—I'm set to hold an interview with Signor Di Pasqua tomorrow! Papà broke the news to me when he came back from his recent trip to Venice, his eyes bright and dancing, his body barely able to keep itself from trembling in excitement.

He's talked about me, apparently, and Signor Di Pasqua actually listened in spite of his busy schedule, and Papà's been bragging about my talent since his first interview with the gentleman several weeks ago.

And now Signor Di Pasqua wishes to see me and discuss the possibility of teaching his ward music because apparently the young man (he's eighteen, which Gilles said before and Papà now confirms) is in need of discipline, having grown up quite spoiled and wild.

Signor Di Pasqua is his maternal grandfather's younger brother, which I suppose I can officially call his granduncle, and the young man (his name's Andrea) was orphaned at an early age and was raised by his grandparents. Apparently, as with all things to do with grandparenting, the boy was spoiled by their indulgence, and now his granduncle has taken him in and is determined to shape his behavior and character with music lessons in addition to other things.

I don't know if I can manage it, I'll admit, but if it means being able to stick close to Papà and be generously paid for my trouble, I'm willing to give it a go. I only hope Andrea won't be the death of me.

Chapter 19

I barely focused on work the next day, my attention constantly zeroing in on Christian whenever he was nearby, and when he wasn't? I'd actually look around for him. It was actually pretty tragic, the way I kept seeking him out and then just following his movements around the warehouse.

One would have thought I'd never seen a boy before, but I couldn't help it. He was way out of my league, and I kept wondering why he'd voluntarily call me and ask me out to a movie and dinner. I couldn't wrap my head around it even though he never once hinted I was being a real pest or, worse, a stalker wannabe.

Maybe he felt sorry after Elliot told him, I thought, ducking my head for the bazillionth time when he walked past my worktable. I at least had my earbuds on and was back to listening to classical music, so I had a crutch—well, an excuse to pretend I didn't notice him though I was sure my face and its vampire complexion was completely splotchy with red.

I didn't blush well and in fact looked more ill than embarrassed when I did.

Whenever I didn't pay too much attention to him, my music drew me away—far away, in fact, even if I'd never been to any of those places I kept picturing in my head. People on horses, people in carriages. Men and women in some pretty elaborate clothing including wigs. Grand palaces—palazzos, I guess, because Venice also kept popping up in my mind.

I'd already stopped fighting against these images and especially the dreams. I figured given how I was responding to the music—and given how the music seemed to be deeply connected somehow to those dreams—it would serve me well if I just let myself go and see where all these would take me.

The one thing I still couldn't quite wrap my head around was San Tadeo church and what had happened to me the last time I went there. With the distance of time, however short, I gradually became aware of the fact that the events might've made me uneasy, but in the end, I wasn't so freaked out that I wouldn't want to go back.

If anything, maybe going back to the church when the Angelus bell rang again would actually help me piece things together and understand just why things were happening now. I had a feeling whatever I needed to know could be found in that church, and the more I considered it, the surer I felt. I blinked, my movements stopping as I chased after that idea with Couperin's music tickling my ears.

"I came out to Mom and Dad," I muttered. "That was when the dreams started—sometime around that."

It made some weird sense, I thought, and with that, I shook things off and carried on with my work. I had time enough tonight to mull over that, but that was one puzzle piece neatly finding its place in a mixed up and still unfinished picture.

When our shift ended, Christian walked up to my table with that amazing smile of his. "So are you still up for later? It's okay if you think you need more time to rest."

"I'm good. I guess I'll see you there, then?"

"Yeah—but earlier." He paused and grimaced, absentmindedly running a hand through his hair. I helplessly watched the soft, straight strands fall back into place, their blunt edges grazing his brows. "Looks like my mom needs me to help her with some stuff tonight. My personal time had to be cut down and moved forward. Sorry."

We were set to meet at four, of all times, but I'd take what I could get at this point though I was pretty disappointed about it. I still had time enough to shower, get dressed properly for a date, and even nap for a few minutes once I got home.

* * * *

I couldn't get enough of him. And judging from the way he took me all the way in, eager and energetic, his fingers digging into my hips while mine kneaded his cheeks as I took him in, neither could he get enough of me. We whimpered and moaned around each other's hard lengths, taking our time with each other while the breeze blew in through the wide-open windows.

Naked and flushed, drenched with sweat from our earlier and ongoing exertions, we both lay in a nest of silk, lace, and velvet, luxuriating in each other's bodies and idle in our pace. We had all the time in the world, I thought as I sucked and licked, delighting in the trembling body I held as Andrea fought off the need to release and rapidly failing in his control. He wasn't alone in that.

The wet sounds of slurping and sucking increased, along with our quiet whimpers and moans, and our bodies writhed and chased after relief with increasing desperation. And when it finally happened, we both came at the same time, flooding each other's throats with warmth and swallowing hungrily.

It took another hazy moment for us to gather ourselves, and Andrea shifted and moved so that we faced each other. I watched him for a bit, lost in wonder and the acute pain of love in my chest, speechless at the idea that this god-like youth had thought me worthy of his body—and his heart as well.

"I love you," he murmured with a soft smile, blue eyes lit with affection, his blond hair feeling like silk against my fingers. I did enjoy caressing him like this during our recovery.

"I love you, too," I murmured back.

"Paolo—let's—let's run away. I know you're worried about your father, but he won't approve of us."

"No one will, darling. I'm afraid—I'm afraid no matter where we go, where we hide, no one will approve of us."

Andrea knew that. He was no fool. And I saw it in the way the light changed in his eyes, the way it dulled in heavy acknowledgment of our reality. It wouldn't be long, I thought, before he'd be pressed to find a woman to marry and sire heirs. He was set to inherit a good bit of money and property from his parents and grandparents, and should his granduncle die, perhaps some of Signor Di Pasqua's wealth would also be bequeathed to him.

Andrea was born to be a prince, I kept thinking, and I wasn't. And should we be caught out, the heavier burden of punishment would surely be on me, and I wouldn't have anywhere to go. Papà was my only refuge, and even then, I doubted if he'd be so forgiving. And if anything, I'd kill my own father simply by breaking his fond heart, and that thought alone was unbearable.

"It isn't fair," he said after a painful pause. I watched him swallow a couple of times as though to ease the tightness in his throat, my heart breaking for him. For both of us. "It isn't. I hate it here, and I hate being forced into music lessons I'm not good at. I wish I were left alone in Modena."

"Then we wouldn't have met, and we wouldn't have fallen in love with each other, right?"

"Don't you think sometimes it would've been better had we not met?"

The words stung, but there was truth in them. Yes, I'd thought about it so many times before as I lay wide awake at night, my heart breaking for both of us. But this was the time we were born into, and we had no choice but be caught in the unruly and unpredictable currents of Fortune.

No matter how I turned things over in my head in search of ways with which we could redirect the paths laid out for us, no answer came. Half the time I'd cry myself to sleep, unable to come to terms with letting Andrea go someday. We'd only found each other. It had only been three months since we first met, and yet he already owned my heart as surely as I owned his.

"Sometimes," I replied, and my eyes burned even as I tried to smile my reassurance. "But I suppose it's better to have met you and fallen in love than never at all."

Andrea nodded, and he quickly rolled on top of me for a long, desperate kiss, quite ready for another round, it seemed. But he was eighteen, I was nineteen, and we had energy and love enough to endure fatigue. Disappointment, surely? No, I thought as I groaned under Andrea's weight and his body's tight heat.

I wanted so much to run away with him, but I was both pragmatic about our chances and terrified of what could happen to us. And when he rode me, face close to mine, I felt the small, wet drops of his tears on my face. Outside the season blessed the city and its canals with its soft breeze, the warmth easing the closer we got to autumn.

* * * *

I awoke from my nap feeling not only tired, but depressed in spirits. It took me some time to get myself together with a quick snack before jumping into the shower, my mind filled with that vivid—overly vivid—dream of me and Andrea together.

I took my umbrella, wallet, and keys, and soon I was heading out the door, the flurry of activity easily pushing the aftereffects of my dream back.

Soon I was walking quickly up the sidewalk toward the discount theater, noting the small and scattered people milling around the ticket booth. I quickly spotted Christian, who saw me first and waved. I had to calm down, I told myself, as I neared him.

"Glad you can come," he said once I neared, almost breathless and grinning stupidly at him. "We were hoping you'd be okay."

We? As though hearing my thoughts, Elliot emerged from the crowd, smiling and holding up three tickets. "I got them," he crowed, eyes dancing behind his glasses, his braces making him look even younger than a high school senior. "Hi, Adam! Good to see you again."

I was able to rally quickly enough, and we were soon walking toward the concession stand. Christian and Elliot started talking, and confusion gripped me as I slowed my pace until I was shadowing them a few steps behind. Christian didn't say anything about Elliot tagging along our date, and while I liked Elliot, I was still mystified by his being there.

Then I looked down and realized they were holding hands, fingers laced. They even wore matching bracelets, and with that, little things started to click in my head—small details and fleeting moments at work. The way Christian always ended up at Elliot's worktable to chat. The way he'd always drop everything to help Elliot with something too big and heavy even though there were other guys in the warehouse who could've done it.

The way they always left for home together, when I thought they were merely ride sharing or just knew each other much longer to hang out after work, watching superhero DVDs or whatnot.

The pain didn't hit me right away because being tangled up in confusion and shock buffered me from feeling it until the moment we took our seats in the theater. Christian and I flanked Elliot, and after settling in, I noticed they still reached out for each other's hands, locking themselves in their bubble of two even though they never ignored me at any time during the movie and even after.

It was all I could do to distract myself with blond hair and blue eyes, however much it hurt.

Chapter 20

1 July, 17—Andrea was meek and pliant today, which helped our lesson along, but it grieved me all the same because it also meant his granduncle had been bullying him again. The two don't get along at all, and Andrea keeps complaining about wishing his family left him alone after his grandparents died.

He'd have been happy and content living quite shut up in Modena, he told me more than once during his petulant fits. He wouldn't have to put up with Signor Di Pasqua's temper and jealousy.

Jealousy? Yes, I thought it was almost funny how Andrea worded it, but there it was. His granduncle was jealous of him because he was set to inherit a vast amount of wealth and property, and he was also very young and beautiful to boot. People ought to be throwing themselves at his feet, but that's a thought I had, not him.

I'd have done it from the moment I first set eyes on him. I'd have thrown myself at his feet like a swooning, lovestruck bumpkin. He's distracted me so much, I haven't been writing in my journal as regularly as I did before though that's also likely because of my exhaustion at the end of the day.

It's been half a month since we started our lessons, and we haven't really progressed as quickly as I'd hoped. Andrea's moods and sulking aren't helping one bit, and I suspect he sometimes does that on purpose to test my temper and drive me to quit my post in a rage.

Sadly he doesn't know me well, and he certainly doesn't know the desperation with which I'd taken Signor Di Pasqua's offer and terms. As I've noted in an earlier journal entry, I'm now being paid double of what Signor Amatorre had given me when he increased my pay. In fact, I've yet to recover from my interview, and Papà's been quite delirious with joy over the gentleman's generosity.

Signor Di Pasqua doesn't strike me as generous, though. I think he simply doesn't care enough for money as long as it's money well-spent, and despite his flaws, he really does want his grandnephew to succeed and flourish in something involving the arts.

"We are a very musical family, signore," he'd said during my interview. "I have cousins and nieces and nephews who've forged their own paths—successful paths, at that—in music. Regardless of how modest or grand their results are, they're still worth taking great pride in. Indeed, one of my nieces is an abbess, and she's written dozens of hymns for the church—just beautiful stuff."

And he expected—or at least hoped—to see Andrea find his feet in music as well in spite of Andrea's protests and arguments to the contrary. Well, sadly for my pupil, I'm not there to kowtow to him even though I'd cut my own hands off if he were to ask it of me. He isn't paying for my time, after all.

That said, I do worry about this fractious relationship he has with Signor Di Pasqua. Neither of them is able to back down and grant the other the courtesy of a concession, no matter how reluctant or small. The gentleman has age and experience going for him, and Andrea has his youth and his reckless energy. And I'm caught in the middle.

Today might have been a good day for our lessons, but given Andrea's fiery and passionate nature, I can't predict tomorrow. At least my time with Jori continues to be the backbone of my days. Andrea can learn a thing or two from a boy almost ten years his junior.

*

4 July, 17—Papà's become Signor Di Pasqua's favorite, it appears, and while the two continue to be separated by wealth and station, they're a great deal friendlier toward each other now. I reckon it's because of the quality of Papà's work as well as his impeccable work ethic, which his temporary assistants have come to emulate.

I've seen Papà soften our employer's harshness when it comes to his dealings with other people, in particular the servants. But not Andrea, though. I do believe signore is playing the role of strict disciplinarian for Andrea's sake, perhaps overcompensating for those years Andrea's grandparents failed to instill restraint and proper conduct in him.

At any rate, I'm awfully pleased to see Papà enjoy himself again, and he's told me several times just how much he's loving his current commission in spite of how arduous it is. Brother Rafael's come around a couple of times already with his pain medication and his sharp tongue, always scolding Papà for subjecting his aging body to such a strenuous task.

"Your father's impossible," Brother Rafael said once, his kindly eyes flashing in exasperation. "Your poor mother ought to be canonized after putting up with this all her life, God rest her soul."

I could only laugh and shrug helplessly. As for Papà, he'd only sing his own praises in answer, which is fair, I suppose, because he truly does magnificent work regardless of his opinion on his employer's tastes, frivolities, and even outright uselessness. I've yet to see his work at the Di Pasqua palazzo since the room is currently closed off from everyone but signore, but I know it's gorgeous.

I've started to notice Andrea watching me keenly, his gaze probing and thoughtful but never in the same way with which Signor Amatorre observed me. I confess to being unnerved by his scrutiny only because I've been doing the same thing, myself, when he's at the harpsichord, and his back's turned or his eyes are angrily fixed on the music sheet in front of him.

Andrea's so beautiful. I'd watch him all day if I could, but I wasn't hired for that. Besides, I'd be the last person he'd flatter with his attention. Perhaps he's simply bored now that he's been stuck in Venice for over a month.

If he really is someone like me who prefers his own gender, he should be disabused of his interest (if any) in me soon enough. He's yet to attend grand balls or anything of the sort, where gentlemen as rich and beautiful as he are in attendance and can easily catch and hold his attention.

*

9 July, 17—Andrea kissed me. I don't even know how it became possible because I've been doggedly keeping him at a safe enough distance ever since I noticed him observing me like a hawk. I'm not so stupid as to abuse my position as a music teacher and encourage any interest he might have nurtured in that stubborn brain of his. Despite my own doomed infatuation with him, I've been able to stay professional and distant every day, and yet...

I'm trying to recall the moment when I let my guard down.

No, he'd manipulated me into ignoring my self-imposed strictures, the brat!

I arrived this morning to a sulky and red-eyed Andrea, who complained yet again about his granduncle's beastly, draconian rules, etc. Then he took it all out on the helpless harpsichord, utterly butchering Couperin and clearly doing it on purpose even though he said he wasn't and that it was unfair of me to accuse him of being so ghastly. I had to stop him by holding one of his hands still when simply ordering him to stop from my safe distance didn't work.

His behavior caught me off my guard and left me reeling, constantly glancing at the double doors of the music room in fear of Signor Di Pasqua barging in and demanding what on earth was going on with all this dreadful noise. For the first time since my hiring, I was truly afraid. I refused to risk this hard-won post over a spoiled brat's tantrums, and my temper got the better of me in the end. So I was forced to march up to him, reach out, and rudely stop him with my hand on his.

It worked, at least, and I all but pushed him off the bench and sat down to demonstrate the correct technique. He knew how to do it; of that I was sure. Little did I realize just how simple a trap he laid out for me, and what I did was exactly what he wished.

I finished playing, my temper soothed a little, and when I turned with a huff to berate him for his childish display, I never got a word out because he'd moved so close to me while I was playing and waited his turn, leaning down and pressing his lips to mine when I looked up at him.

I froze while he kissed me, stunned speechless and left immobile while my brain suddenly failed to function. Andrea didn't care; in fact, once I stopped moving altogether, he pressed on, never releasing me and managed to slip his tongue between my slack lips and inside my mouth, where he indulged himself for a few seconds. Several seconds.

And I let him. In the end, I was so transfixed by what he was doing that I simply allowed it to happen and go on until he pulled away with such care and gentleness that only added to my shock.

He even smiled—a soft, tender smile—his mouth pinker than before.

"Thank you for putting up with me," he simply whispered. Then he kissed me on the nose and straightened up, adjusted his wig, and strode out of the music room. Apparently our lesson was done though it hadn't been an hour yet, and he never returned.

I don't remember how long I stuck around, sitting like an idiot at the harpsichord and just gaping into space. At least none of the servants came by and caught me doing that, but my brain finally came out of its catatonia, and I was obliged to move though I did so on shaky knees and faltering limbs. I gathered my books and music sheets and all but fumbled my way out of the music room.

Signor Di Pasqua was nowhere in sight, for which I was grateful, but his secretary met me somewhere (again the details are still blurry even after a few hours since), thanked me graciously for my time, and presented me with this month's pay.

I don't expect Papà to be back from Venice for another day, which isn't a good thing for me at the moment as I've got no one to talk to and distract me, and writing all of this down in my journal is only adding to the wild jumble of thoughts in my head. Such thoughts are things one ought not to discuss in polite company or in any company whatsoever unless they were with their lover.

Andrea shouldn't have done it. He shouldn't have. I'd accuse him of abusing his position as my pupil and superior in station, but that would mean admitting I didn't want it nor welcome it. If anything, he did exactly as I'd always fantasized, and he was chaste about it compared to my fraught imaginings.

He didn't bend down and offer his body to me, and neither did he drape himself out on a piece of furniture in open invitation for a thorough fucking. But he'd still managed to shatter a dam with one kiss, and nothing after this will turn out well. No, this isn't good. Virgin, give me strength!

Chapter 21

I woke up with a pained sound that was more like a suppressed sob. It only took me a handful of seconds to reorient myself and saw I was in my bedroom, and a glance at my old digital clock—a relic inherited from my grandparents—told me there had been a power outage while I slept. The clock face flashed one-twenty-seven, which meant the power just got back on almost an hour and a half ago.

Thunder rolled outside, the rain matching its attitude in the way the city got hammered. I scrubbed my face with both hands, my dream barely holding on to remind me what it had been. It would only take a few more seconds for it to flutter away into the night in a hundred little pieces.

Andrea, I thought. I'd dreamt of Andrea, but it had been more like representative images than actual scenes like before.

I remembered him quietly walking up to me, and I was lying down on something hard. I couldn't remember whatever else might have been going on around us, but I could still see him kneeling down beside me, crying hard. I'd touched his face with one hand, gently stroking his cheek while he sobbed, and when he turned his head slightly, I saw a mark on his throat.

A bruise—not of fingers, but a line across, dark enough for me to see and realize it was a mark made by a rope or whatever it was he'd used to hang himself with. I tried to talk but found I couldn't move my mouth even though I was still able to stroke his wet face, my own heart breaking over and over again, hopeless anguish twisting my insides and making me wail in my head.

I touched my own throat at the memory, the need to use the bathroom forcing me to get up and stop fixating on a horrible dream. I suppose I had time enough to do that, anyway.

The actual time was just after five in the morning, apparently, which I discovered downstairs. I should have gone back to bed, but I was still rattled by the dream and tried to have something to eat instead. It was Saturday then, and my parents would be back home the next weekend.

And as I gloomily ate a croissant with tea, I wondered what to say to them once they were back or, worse, how to behave around them. My conversation with them last night still haunted me with Dad fishing around with leading questions and Mom being passive-aggressive in her hints.

"There are a few people here who talked about how alone they are now and how worried they are when old age comes. Who's going to take care of them? They don't have grandchildren who'll cheer them up, and I know just how important that is when you're nearing the end of your time on earth, and you grow more aware of your life and the people—if any—surrounding you," Mom said.

"Couples can always adopt, you know."

"I know that. But some of these people are gay or lesbian."

"If I ever get married or something to another man, we can adopt. There's also surrogacy, and I know how pricey that can be, but that's still an option. It's not like I'm cursed to grow old and die lonely, Mom."

"Tell *that* to those who talked to us about their bad life choices."

"How's work coming along, son?" Dad asked in that tone of voice of his that pretty much heralded a dreaded interrogation. "How are the people you work with?"

"I really like them," I said honestly. "They're really nice to me and have been patient and understanding."

It was true—I really liked everyone at work for the first time since I started applying for jobs. We all looked after each other, and our supervisors and especially Curtis made sure we were all safe and not overextending ourselves even though we still ran into problems and a random disaster. They made sure to calm us down and coax us off the ledge, even send us home if the situation called for it.

"Have you met anyone you like?"

Had I met anyone I fancied, he meant, and my chest ached at the reminder of Christian and Elliot and that horrible time I had at the theater. But whose fault was that, anyway, but mine? I'd been the one to feed my own embarrassing daydreams about Christian and how beautiful he was and how friendly he was toward me.

I should have known better, I kept telling myself, and stopped myself from chasing after unfounded things, but maybe that was loneliness manifesting itself.

And when I spoke with Dad over the phone last night, and he asked me that question, I had to fight back the tears and spent the rest of my conversation with him swiping my eyes with the back of my hand. Because I *was* lonely. I'd had crushes over the years, and once I came out to myself before my parents, that awareness of other boys sharpened. Checking out different online sites for people like me helped out, but that didn't make my wish for someone to love any less pressing.

If anything, when the dreams and broken nights of sleep started after I came out, that wish—that desire—seemed to have morphed into something else that was a hundred times worse because now it felt more like loving profoundly once and then losing it. If my dreams were anything to go by—and if past lives were really a thing and I was slowly awakening to mine—it had been a traumatic ordeal for me. I'd loved deeply maybe because I was young and painfully naïve about so many things still. And just as profoundly, I'd lost everything.

But tell that to my parents, especially Dad. I couldn't explain anything to myself. How the hell would I manage it with my parents?

"I met someone I like, Dad," I said after a quick hesitation.

"Oh?" His tone wasn't encouraging. It was incredible, really, just how much a person revealed themselves with the way they said just one word.

"But he's already involved with someone else."

"Hmm. Hopefully not an open relationship. We had long conversations with some of our new friends here about that trend, and it's no wonder gay men get sick."

Dad likely meant get sick with AIDS or whatever the epidemic of the decade in the gay community happened to be, which had been a cause for concern for him and Mom when I came out to them. Would I be so wild with other guys and catch some gay-only disease?

I'd quickly shut them both down when they raised the issue, and they hadn't said anything about it since, but now that they were away from me and were constantly surrounded by other conservative Catholics and possibly gay people who regretted their life choices, I was afraid they were going to throw all of that back in my face.

Between my stupidity toward Christian and last night's phone call with Mom and Dad, I found I didn't have an appetite for dinner and cried myself to sleep. It was a good thing it was the weekend, and I wasn't going to show up to work looking like death warmed over.

The six o'clock bell for the early morning Angelus rang, and I didn't even think about it. I placed all of my used dishes in the sink for washing later, dressed up for bad weather, snatched my umbrella and keys, and was soon braving the downpour and thunder. The streets were silent and still though I saw a few lit windows in houses and apartments I passed.

A fleeting memory was triggered then: blond hair, blue eyes wide and startled. Heavy rain, a stammered apology. I almost tripped as another surge of intense emotion gripped me, but I had to shake it off. I needed to be somewhere quick.

San Tadeo church looked its hoped-for age in the darkness and rain, only the light from the street lamps helping it stay visible. I paused at the bottom of the front steps and looked up, feeling older than the church. Every step I took closer weighed on me and made me more aware of my unique and maybe even terrifying position, straddling different centuries if what I deduced from my dreams and odd flashbacks were true.

The doors were unlocked, and the moment I entered the silent church, I felt the quiet shift in time. It was the same old mission church I grew up attending masses in, a sanctuary for everyone, one that now felt so ancient. Timeless, even. Every familiar detail now seemed just beyond my reach, recognizable and yet not, weighed down and slowly bending under long-forgotten memories.

The door didn't make a sound when I opened and closed it, of course, but that didn't stop me. The interior was again softly lit by the old chandeliers and wall sconces.

Instead of heading down the aisle toward the front of the nave, though, I turned right and walked straight for the side chapel. It was also dimly lit by a couple of sconces, the votive candles long guttered. The small, private space dedicated to the Virgin Mary felt unreal—eerie. The statue's small, calm smile and its downturned gaze alternately beckoned to me and repulsed me, and the closer I got to it, the more my hair rose until my knees locked completely, and I was suddenly fixated on the stone floor directly in front of the shrine.

Panic now roiled in my belly, my heart thundering and my breaths growing shallower and faster as I stared in confused horror at the floor. There was nothing wrong with it. It was well-maintained and clean, a single prie-dieu standing in front of the alcove containing the Virgin's statue. It was a simple and humble little space of private devotion, and yet the longer I stayed there, the more I was gripped by some irrational dread and fear.

"Open yourself. No one else will do it for you," I whispered over and over until my knees unlocked, and I took painful, jerking steps toward the prie-dieu. Just as slowly and jerkily I knelt on it, but my gaze was still fixed on the stone floor, not the statue.

Something had happened there, I realized, an icy wave rolling through me. My hair continued to stand on end as ghostly impressions flittered past my mind—barely there for me to hold on to, moving too quickly and sharply for me be anything but puzzled.

Fragmented images, jagged pieces of a shattered mirror from the past—a wildly spinning room like this side chapel, a jolting view of the Madonna, and a sharp turning of the world around me, the stone floor flying at me at an unnatural speed. And the awful, awful pain shooting through my head...

I didn't realize I'd slid off the prie-dieu and placed myself before the Virgin with both hands on the cold floor, my face pressed against it, my body shuddering under a torrent of loud sobs. I died here. With a certainty I couldn't explain and couldn't measure, I knew. I died here, and my soul, aging in centuries, howled.

Chapter 22

23 July, 17—Andrea was at his best behavior today because Signor Di Pasqua thought to sit in on our lesson, determined to see for himself if my pupil's improved after a few weeks of working with him. I still haven't told signore just how slow-going it's been with Andrea compared to Jori or even Maddalena.

Motivation certainly accounts for the difference in results, but I think I'll also throw in age as a factor. Children, especially those with proven gifts in music, are more likely to catch on and absorb new techniques. I know Signor Belluomo, bless his soul, praised me to the heavens in front of my parents whenever they came by after each lesson, saying he's never worked with a child so talented and gifted before.

I remember advancing so quickly in our lessons and sometimes leaving the poor old gentleman at a bit of a loss as to how best to fill up what was left of our time. We'd play together, in fact, in a burst of spontaneous fun, dueling on the harpsichord or simply playing a duet written by an unknown talent long gone. And those moments always felt so good, defining some of the happiest memories I have of my childhood.

My poor teacher! If only he could see me now! Would he be disappointed in my work? I suppose I can always reassure him I'm the youngest music teacher in these parts though I can't say for sure if there are others like me elsewhere.

One barrier I've had in securing work has been my age, in fact, because some people are convinced only older music teachers are equipped to pass on their knowledge of music to the next generation, and I understand their meaning. I'm fortunate enough to convince some families that my age will benefit their children more because they'd be less intimidated.

But I've clearly strayed from the point of this entry with thoughts I've recorded over and over again. I suppose it's truly a sore point with me than I've cared to admit if I can't seem to let such matters go in my journal.

Signor Di Pasqua sat in on our lessons today, and Andrea was very much the ideal pupil if only for show. He was polite but spirited, asking questions and answering questions from start to finish. By the time we reached the end, we still had a few minutes to spare, and signore—clearly in a state of melancholy reverie—produced an old document, which turned out to be an original composition for the harpsichord.

"I'd be most obliged if you or Andrea would play it for me," the gentleman said in a surprisingly quiet and restrained manner. Gone were his energy and overt displays of deep pride in his reputation, family, and property, his stubbornness in demanding perfection.

Andrea was good enough in sight-reading, but he's still nowhere near my ability, and he humbly surrendered the harpsichord to me and took his place nearby to watch.

I played it—it was a sweet, easy enough piece to read, and it was clearly written by an amateur with a deep love for music. It sounded almost like a lullaby with its gently swaying rhythm and moderate pacing, and when I was done, I found signore staring through me, his mind very much far, far from the present and perhaps even Venice.

"That was my niece's composition," he said at length, his voice just as quiet and sad as before. "Andrea's mother, I mean. She didn't have aspirations for music, but she loved it, and she wrote that for her son. I didn't know I still had it hidden away all this time and came upon it while sorting out some important documents last night."

His gaze cleared, and he turned to Andrea with a solemn nod and a quick wave of a hand at me.

"She'd want you to have this, Andrea. She wrote it for you. You can even read the dedication on the piece, and perhaps you'll be inspired to learn it and master it—for her sake. I suppose that's one way of keeping her memory alive. She wrote quite a few pieces over the years, you know. Most of them were meant for you and your father. Given what I've seen today, it appears you're more than ready to honor them both by learning them and filling this room with their spirits with your skillful playing. Signor Agnelli, I'm quite impressed with what you've accomplished with Andrea so far. Well, done, young man."

He then rose and left without another word and without waiting for either of us to speak. I didn't think it was necessary, anyway, and Andrea took the music sheets from me in what appeared to be numbed silence, kissing me distractedly and then leaving as well.

We don't have lessons tomorrow, but we're set to meet at a friend's home in Treviso and spend the day together. He's growing bolder, my Andrea, but I'd be lying if I said I'm not relieved. For all his fire and impetuousness, he's a very caring and selfless lover, awfully patient with me in bed.

I suppose this is where our worlds converge. Music and love—the music room and the bedroom—one will forever be the teacher, and even Andrea's all but stopped his rebellious turns on the harpsichord. He's just pleased to spend a small amount of time with me nearly every day, I think, and perhaps that's influencing his progress as well.

*

30 July, 17—The warmth and lazy days of summer are quite powerful, I find. I'm more sluggish in mind and body though Andrea ensures my energy never goes to waste when we're together. He's everything to me now, and I sometimes pause in what I'm doing whenever a stray thought finds its way to the front of my mind, and my vision's suddenly filled with Andrea and a random moment I spent in his company.

Not so much in bed, either, because almost all of my happiest memories of him revolve around more mundane moments spent walking down the narrow lanes linking *campi* together or enjoying food and drink in a coffeehouse or simply watching the water from an unpopular and less visited spot somewhere away from civilization.

Whenever we're alone outside, we try to sit closer together, with Andrea sometimes bringing an extra coat as a prop, so he could use it to hide our joined hands while we enjoy some quiet time gazing out at the endless sea and watching the sun creep across the sky.

Within doors, my favorite moments would be those of us simply holding each other close—not kissing necessarily though that certainly adds special flavor to the moment, but enclosing each other in our arms. I particularly love holding Andrea so that his face is gently pressed against my shoulder since I'm taller than he, and I cradle the back of his head with one hand. It's a protective embrace, I guess, and I know my love for him only grows stronger, which makes such a hold all the more meaningful.

I do wonder sometimes if Papà ever held Mamma the same way. Up until the end, after so many years together, they were so deeply in love, with their bond reshaping itself from the wild passion of youth to something subtler yet stronger and more lasting. I hope I'm able to achieve the same with Andrea in spite of our age.

Other people might argue that we're still far too young and unable to see the world and especially reality with a clearer and more judicious eye. That is, if society actually viewed our love for each other the same way they viewed the love between a man and a woman.

There are too many things going against us. I know that too well. I live with it every day, and I'm now even more convinced Papà will die without seeing me married and blessing him with grandchildren. So many obstacles, so many unjust laws—all I want is for me and Andrea to be given a fair chance at love. That's all.

I've prayed for it—so many times now, and I only hope the Virgin is listening and is willing to intercede on our behalf the way she's always interceded for everyone else over time. I don't know if I'll be deemed good enough to be granted such a wish, so for now I'll hold my Andrea close at every opportunity, be lost in the pain of love when we're in bed.

*

3 August, 17—Andrea turned nineteen today, and we celebrated with a rather spirited lesson with him in such a good mood. The solemnity of exercises and new pieces to learn went right out the window, but with so many strictures relaxed for today, Andrea's joy and love of music (in spite of his lack of a motivation for developing his skill) expressed itself so freely in spontaneous magic on the harpsichord.

We played Scarlatti from start to finish, Andrea not at all minding being corrected and ordered to start over. His exuberance compelled me to throw the windows of the music room wide open—all of them, in fact—and allow the warm sea breeze to blow right inside while letting music float out and away. With any luck, anyone outside enjoyed it. I certainly did, my heart clenching at the sight of my pupil actually loving every moment coaxing some of the most intricate and beautiful music out of an instrument he usually despised.

He knows my fondness for the Sonata in D minor, and he played it for me without hesitation, appearing to love every key, every trill. He even led me away from the harpsichord and pressed me to sit by one of the windows and simply be entertained.

"I love you," he whispered when he fussed over me even after I was seated, drawing a tender smile from me. "I wish I could do more than this, but this ought to mean something."

"This is more than enough, Andrea," I whispered back once reassured of the double doors remaining shut against the household. "You know all I want for you is to be happy."

"I *am* happy—when I'm with you, I'm deliriously happy, and I can only hope for forever." He kissed me before walking back to the harpsichord to delight me with his mastery, however limited, of the pieces we've gone through together.

From start to finish, he performed for me, expressing his heart with the impulsive passion he's always displayed, no matter what his mood. And today, his birthday made him soar higher than I've ever seen, and I thought of Icarus and his defiant flight to the sun.

I suppose that would also include me—Icarus would be us together, equipped with wings of wax, taking flight toward the blinding glory of the sun, heedless and perhaps reckless in our joyful abandonment now that we've found each other and hold each other's hearts so closely. I also couldn't help but think about Papà then—so hard at work elsewhere in the palazzo, determined to prove to his temporary employer just how good he is in fresco-work and equally determined to ensure my security and happiness.

Look, Papà! I'm in love and am loved back! I can now understand just how wonderful and perfect life had been with Mamma, and I hope you don't begrudge me my heart's choice.

Andrea's wild energy was infectious, and even so many hours after, I'm still flying. Perhaps our wings are stronger, after all, because I've never felt so hopeful in my life. The sun's rays draw near, but I don't care.

Chapter 23

So many images, so many sounds—all broken and nearly incoherent yet filling so many deep, impenetrable spaces in my head. Andrea—my beloved, beautiful Andrea—smiling, weeping, raging, lost in the heights of passion while he rides me or while I fuck him to completion. His taste when I kiss him fervently or softly, his responsiveness where I was concerned either with touch or speech, so that everything he did was shaped—sometimes to the point of grotesque distortion—by his heart. I loved him so much, it hurt to think of him, and I did think of him even as I lay in bed, waiting for sleep to come.

Even when I sat across the table from Papà while he prodded me for information. Rumors were beginning to circulate among the servants, he said with a worried look in my direction. *Is it true, Paolo? What they're whispering—is it true?* I felt his confusion and anger on my behalf. I could tell he refused to believe the nonsense spouted by the signore's servants, which his temporary workers were in danger of hearing as well.

Servants will always gossip, Papà. I don't know why you bothered to listen to them. I didn't lie to him, but I didn't answer him with the naked truth, either. Andrea's eagerness to spend his time with me completely was intensifying, his irritability when it came to his granduncle's strictures and sermons, escalating to the point where he wasn't caring at all anymore.

We fought again, Paolo. This time he's threatening to send me to Paris to study under some wretched old windbag who once taught some wretched old composer something or other. He said I'm not improving quickly enough for him. He's trying to break us up—I hate him so much!

Images and words spun in a terrifying whirlwind, blending into each other, impressing on me more and more that my memories were returning to me, stumbling over each other in their hurry to find their long-forgotten places. Present and past collided, fought for supremacy, and fell away from each other as each reclaimed their places in my head and my heart.

Andrea? Where is he, Papà? What have they done with him? Andrea!

Stop it! Stop it now! How could you do this to me and your poor mother? What possessed you to destroy everything we built for you? All this sacrifice on your account for a better life than we ever had—gone! And for what?

Don't touch me! I have to see him! Andrea! No, stop it! I'm not praying with you!

Kneel before her, by God! Pray! She'll help you cleanse your soul! She'll forgive you if you humble yourself to her! Stop fighting me, Paolo! Stop it now! Kneel!

No! I won't! Let me go! No! N—

I came to then, my head clear and pain-free by some miracle. The rain pummeled the city, the thunder still rumbling in the early morning hours. I realized I was lying on one of the pews at the rear of the church, which was still empty and silent—no, not empty, I thought as I looked around me with a strangely keener awareness of my surroundings.

Not empty. There was someone praying all the way in the front, in one of the pews nearest the altar. He had his back to me, and his head was bowed, so I didn't dare disturb him from such a private moment.

I glanced back to the entrance of the side chapel, and I knew instantly I needed to go back there. I rose, feeling no ache or even stiffness at all, a surge of—what, energy? Life?—coursing through me like fresh blood. I felt hope, but it also seemed to have been woven from the frayed and faded threads of profound sorrow. Once I reached the side altar's entrance, I saw the man whom I'd seen a few days ago while I was trying to flee San Tadeo church in a panic. He stood before the Virgin's statue lost in thought, his gaze fixed on her and yet not.

"Papà," I said quietly, and the man turned to me.

In the light of that side chapel, his features revealed themselves to me, lines of insurmountable grief and a burdened conscience throwing harsh shadows on a gaunt, tired face. He regarded me in silence for a brief moment before turning and nodding at the statue's base.

"You died there," he said. "You fought me hard, and I fought back—hit you hard enough for you to fall against the base and crack your skull open. There was so much blood, and she saw everything. So much blood."

"It was an accident. You didn't mean to hurt me."

"You were our pride and joy, Paolo. Our own blessed little musician, we used to call you, bound for great things. I never thought your dreams would end at nineteen. Or that I'd be the cause of that." He raised his right hand and looked at it as though it were some foreign object that baffled him. "I never hit you in anger or in punishment, even when you were at your worst as a child. But when I did—that one time—dear God, what a price."

He didn't cry the whole time we talked. I'd a feeling he'd spent all those centuries in some terrible limbo of his or God's making, crying for what he'd done, waiting for the right time for me to come to him, allow him the chance to rest. Maybe he'd spent that time praying, begging for absolution from the woman whose presence he'd blasphemed with my blood.

"I'm all right now, Papà. I'm alive and well. Things are different today than they were then, and—well—whatever happens with my family now won't end up as badly as before." I chewed my lip and looked at the Virgin, faintly marveling at her odd, otherworldly beauty. "They're also Catholics—pretty conservative types. So my life now isn't as different as the one before in that sense, I guess. But I've got another chance this time."

"Better late than never, as they say." He glanced at me and cracked a wan smile.

"You being here right now—was this her doing?" I indicated the Virgin with my head.

"Maybe. I can't say. This was my idea and mine alone. I bargained with everything above—anyone who'd listen—for another chance. I suppose I was mad enough to do so, but someone had told me before that it's only a man's will that defines his limits."

That sounded rather blasphemous, I thought with a bit of amusement, but I stayed quiet.

"It was my will, I suppose, that I'd not find real rest until we met again in some way or another. I'm bound to any space like this, where my child was baptized and where he died at my hands. I waited for you to come back, and you did—again and again, through the centuries. I'd watch you say different prayers in different languages, weeping and alone, begging for guidance that never came.

"But each time wasn't right, you know. I needed you to step out, embrace yourself the way you did back in Venice, find strength to move forward and not hide back in the shadows out of fear. Sometimes I wondered if I was the one who'd put that fear in you, given what had happened, and it haunted your days, one lifetime after another." He sighed, his head drooping to his chest, though I think he went back to looking at the spot where I'd hit my head. "Each century was different, of course. Today's a much easier time for you to discover yourself and welcome what you see. What you can't change."

"And that's the only way for me to come back to you."

"It shows triumph, I suppose. Progression. Peace of mind. The comforting idea that my only child will be happy at last. I hated the fact that you died miserable—frightened and upset, probably convinced I despised you completely. What parent in his right mind would wish that for his child?" He chuckled, shaking his head. "Only a monster would."

"I forgive you."

He looked up and turned to face me. "Your mother and I have always been very proud of you, you know. Even if we didn't understand then, but I do now. It took me centuries, but I learned so much."

I nodded. "I know. And you've done your best for me, Papà. Thank you."

He pulled me close, and we embraced for a while, surrounded by a peace I'd never ever experienced in a church before. We released each other reluctantly, and he kissed my cheek. I felt dampness, and when he pulled away for the last time, he was smiling through his tears.

"God be with you, Paolo. I'm off to my rest now."

"I love you, Papà. Thank you for everything."

"I love you, too, son. Now go to him and move on with your life. My work's done, and I'm very tired." And with a gentle push, he forced my feet, and I walked back out to the main church, down the center aisle, and toward him. Toward Andrea, who now stood by the pew where he'd been praying and was now watching me with wary hope. My strides lengthened and quickened till I was all but running to him, and with a frantic sob, I fell into his arms and held him so tightly before God, spinning in a stumbling circle while he held me just as tightly back, his own tears soaking my jacket.

Blond hair, blue eyes wide and startled, a stammered apology in the unforgiving rain. Beyond all hope, I found him again, and I'd be damned if I let him go.

When we released each other, I couldn't talk for a moment—just cry and drink him in with eyes swimming in tears while my hands shook and touched his face, his hair, familiarizing themselves with all of him. Andrea did the same with me, and my heart tightened by the raw wonder in his face as he mirrored my disbelief and my unspeakable joy in finding each other again. My fingers grazed his throat, and I took a shuddering breath.

"Why did you have to kill yourself? I saw you—in my dreams, you had a rope mark here."

"Because you were already dead," he said, his voice just as thick as mine. "He told me you died, and he didn't even care. That old fucker even smirked when he told me. I couldn't live with it. I couldn't."

So I kissed him, and he kissed me back, and we both reached out for each other across time and across continents, our hearts seeking their lost partners under such impossible odds, but it had been time and patience that slowly eroded the barriers that had kept us apart for too long.

With Papà's help, with the Virgin's intercession, perhaps—whatever miracle had taken place behind this final coming together, it had done so for me, unbelievable though it might sound. Me. A prodigy constrained badly by poverty, born with his own faults but still deemed to be deserving of perfect happiness in the arms of a young man who loved, perhaps too much.

"I go by Luke now," he murmured as I held him close like I used to as we stood in damp clothes in that silent church, his head cradled against my shoulder. "And I'm hungry for some breakfast."

Chapter 24

17 August, 17—I haven't been dedicating a lot of time (or my usual allotment of time) writing in my journal. I know I've complained about this before, and I did try to be more judicious, but I've failed every time.

This new post in Venice has left me dreadfully exhausted at the end of the day that I simply can't manage to do more than prepare food for dinner, clean, and do a half-hearted attempt at washing myself before tumbling into bed. I've also been very fortunate to have received inquiries for an interview for a possible post in Rome: a teaching position at a small academy for music, a newly established one, too, that's a charity effort for poor but promising students. Children like me, I suppose, who've shown talent and simply need a chance to have that talent nurtured and shaped.

It was Signora Tessaro who facilitated everything—and all the way from Paris, at that. She'd used her connections to forward my name with recommendations, and apparently Signor Cloutier was also asked about me. Signora Salvaggio had also vouched for my skills, and I'm nearly in tears writing this.

People have been very kind to me when all I did was teach their children how to play the harpsichord well. Papà's been dancing and singing since I broke the news to him, and he encourages me to go although for now, I'm trying to save enough money for the trip.

I'm trying not to get my hopes up too much since this is just an interview, but this post will surely mean a steadier income for me. My heart's crushed over the possibility of me leaving and parting ways with the Cloutier family, but at least with Andrea, he's so well-traveled that he's not just excited for me, but also willing to pack his things and move with me.

"We can finally get away from my granduncle's shadow," he said. "I'm so proud of you, darling."

I dare not think more upon this, but I admit it's this prospect I'm quite giddy about. I refuse to spend too much time lost in a fantasy world if I can help it, though, even if no real barrier to that happening has even reared its head to me.

Why, even Signor Di Pasqua's expressed his support—wholehearted, in fact, and perhaps disproportionately so. I've never seen so much excitement in such a stern and rigid person before, but that might just be me. Indeed, if I were to go further, I'd say he even seemed relieved by the news from the way he pressed me, but my imagination does run away with me at times.

*

26 August, 17—My good fortune continues. My request for an interview date has been accepted, and it's set for next week. The academy's so new, in fact, that they're still putting together a faculty and a solid curriculum though they already have a physical location for it. I can't wait to see it!

Andrea had to be convinced to stay behind for now since our trip to Rome together will surely raise suspicions—or raise them further, it appears. Already rumors are circulating among the servants about me dallying with him, and that's making me very nervous.

I suppose that would be something to temper my excitement over my trip. Papà and I have had a few arguments about those rumors already, and I've tried my best to convince him not to listen to anyone without lying and without implicating myself. Papà trusts me too much to see through my prevarications, however, which grieves me all the same because now I'm learning to bend and twist language to save my skin and keep him from a broken heart.

I don't even know what he'd do if I did admit to my relationship with Andrea. Perhaps pull me immediately out of Venice before signore decides to have me arrested or perhaps even flogged (by him) for corrupting Andrea.

Andrea's been roused by these rumors, naturally, and his temper's been short whenever we're together for his lessons. Oh, he still manages to play well enough, but there's a defiance in his performance, and he sometimes attacks the keyboard as though the harpsichord stood for his granduncle, and he's determined to destroy it. I suppose one can say the instrument does stand for Signor Di Pasqua, and our attitudes toward it is emblematic of our relationship with the gentleman.

Those rumors have also forced Andrea's hand, and we haven't been spending as much time together as we'd like, which further puts him out of sorts. "It isn't fair! Why would idle gossip dictate how I love? This is stupid and intolerable! I love you, Paolo! If that old bastard boots you from the premises, I'll kill myself—I swear it!"

His words and the fury and passion with which he spoke them terrified me, of course, and since we were arguing in the music room, I really couldn't do anything to hush him even if I knew he needed me to hold him in reassurance. I can't even remember how our lesson that day turned out because my mind was rattled enough to barely be aware of what we were doing. I simply went through the moves, caught in the currents like a dead leaf.

We can hold off on our trysts until after I leave, and we can then plan his own freedom. He's an heir to a great fortune, anyway, so he's got far more independence than I can ever dream of. He'll be able to pack up and simply leave and have his way, I suppose. Signor Di Pasqua might rant and rave and disown him, but Andrea's already got his parents' and grandparents' wealth to live in luxury for the rest of his life.

I do hope—God, I really do hope—he doesn't tire of me when we're finally together. I hope he doesn't realize what a terrible catch I am with my ragged suits and lack of money.

Winning that academy post, though, would surely put me in a much better position to say I'm deserving of his love (which I still can't believe I've somehow earned) and am not at all useless and likely to live like a parasite off his wealth. Once I'm independent enough, things will fall into place. I'm sure of it.

*

30 August, 17—I can barely write. I don't know what to do. Signor Di Pasqua sacked me today after barging into the music room and catching me kissing Andrea to comfort him because he appeared drunk and raging. They'd had a massive quarrel over breakfast, and it seemed to have been building up for a few days now, he said. Quiet arguments turned into louder ones, and last night, dishes were broken as the two nearly fell upon each other, and frantic servants had to pull them away.

And what a horrible, horrible scene it was in the music room! Signore appeared, a couple of trembling servants behind him, and he was silent in his fury though everyone could tell he was close to murdering someone. He held a walking-stick, the sight of which nearly made my knees buckle because I knew he intended to use it. Andrea, however, goaded him on in his drunken rage, teetering and rumpled, red-faced and without his wig.

"I love Paolo, you fucking goat! But you'll never understand it because you've never loved anyone in your life!" he cried, his words all but lost in signore's own howls of outrage.

There was so much confusion and movement, and I tried to placate both with pleas and a desperate resignation, but signore wouldn't hear of it because he needed the satisfaction of sacking me instead. So he sacked me and ordered his half-fainting servants to escort me out of the premises, and all the while I struggled against them when I heard the shouts in the music room get mixed up with breaking ceramic pieces.

Signore was going to beat Andrea with that stick, I kept thinking, and I fought the servants all the way to the door, my music sheets and books left behind.

"No! He'll hurt him!" I kept crying, but the servants merely begged me to leave, and more servants were summoned when I all but went mad on them, hitting and kicking and doing my best to go back to my Andrea.

Papà was inconsolable, and he's just as furious as signore when he came home for dinner. He's lucky he still has the commission since he's already well into it, and signore likes his work. But his reputation's ruined now, and he's worried sick about finding other work because of what happened today.

Signor Di Pasqua's a very influential man, and a word from him will ruin our chances forever, which means that teaching post in Rome is even more important than ever. But I keep thinking of Andrea, and I'm sick from worry. I hope he's all right. I hope he wasn't beaten. But Papà doesn't know, and he doesn't care. He wants me to pray—to go to church and pray. I've never seen him so angry with me before.

"How could you do this? How could you do this to your poor mother? Have you any idea how hard we've worked for you? How many sacrifices we made on your account? You've thrown it all away, and for what?" That's close to what I remember him saying, but my mind's too burdened right now, and I'm still shaking and frantic.

I'll pick up my pen later. He's knocking on my door now and furiously demanding I go with him to church. I'd rather see Andrea, though. I want to see for myself he's all right and not hurt. I don't want to pray! I don't!

*

My dearest Signor Agnelli,

I'm extremely pleased to hear you've written to Don Ottavio regarding the new post. I hope you're given the position, but judging from what I'm hearing, the recommendations from your former employers are weighing heavily in your favor. Don't be nervous or afraid of the interview as I expect it to be not much more than a ceremonial thing, if you will.

You'll love Rome, and you'll especially love the children. Forgive me for being so thoughtlessly eager on your account and writing you with so much excited chatter on your future. The children aren't just talented and constrained by poverty—all of them are orphans who've displayed some unique talent in music that's caught the nuns' and nurses' attention. I do believe there's one who's very much like you, signore, whose staggering gift in easily playing back music he hears just once is the talk of many academics.

My new post as governess allows me to mingle with such a group as the family I now work for is a family of scholars and professors. That they'd find me suitable for their young children is a miracle in and of itself, and they even listened to me when the subject of this new charitable academy for music came up! I gave them your name, of course, for who else is best suited to teach such young, impressionable minds? You have a rare talent, signore, and you have a kind and generous heart. I know you've talked about your parents' dreams of seeing you made into court composer or something like that, but it appears God has other plans for you, after all. You, Signor Agnelli, are destined to shape the future of Italy's music, and I'm honored to know you.

Good luck in your interview, and do come and visit when you're in Rome! I travel there on occasion with my new family, you see. We shall have good coffee and conversation again!

Ines Tessaro

Chapter 25

Luke and I stopped at the side chapel on our way out and discovered it empty. I wasn't surprised, really. Papà had suffered far too much for far too long, and the Virgin finally called him home. We took a few minutes to pray for his soul before leaving San Tadeo church. The storm carried on all this time, and we shivered outside the church doors for a moment as we decided where to go for breakfast.

"Good heavens! What on earth are you two doing here?" a voice cried.

We turned and found Ms. Garza struggling up the wet stairs, bundled against the storm but still soaking wet.

"There's no service at this time! And the church is locked!"

"But—we were just in it," Luke protested, which drew a look of wry amusement from Ms. Garza.

"No, really. He's not lying." I went to the double doors to open them and found them locked. I blinked and tried again. It was completely secured and unmoving. "Wait..."

"You two need to go home. It's terrible out here." She held up a set of keys and shook them, completely ignoring my confusion. "I've got the keys to the church, see? There's no way anyone can get inside. Now if you'll excuse me, I have to check for leaks in the balcony. That organ's going to cost us our souls if a leak fucks it up."

My house was closer, so I convinced Luke to have breakfast with me, which turned out to be a wise move since we at least had access to towels, a working heater, and even a laundry area. I got Luke to get out of his soaked clothes, dry himself, and temporarily wear an old hoodie and sweatpants of mine while waiting for his clothes to dry. I got us some breakfast, and we sat in the living room—on the rug before the unused fireplace while the heater eased our shivering.

How did one catch up with the love of his life after centuries had passed? Luke told me he had his flashbacks and nightmares roughly a month before I did, and he'd already been visiting San Tadeo by the time I went there and heard echoes of myself praying and crying.

"I've never been a religious person," he said with a little smile and a shrug. "I went there because something told me you were going to show up at any moment. I didn't go every day, but I did whenever my dreams told me to." He looked at me now, a tender light in his eyes. "I didn't know what you'd look like in this lifetime, but I recognized you—your soul, I mean. We look a little different from how we were back then, but I know you. I could tell."

It was true. Luke right now had a lot of similarities to how he looked in my dreams—but only enough for anyone to argue against his identity, which went beyond appearances. Because I did recognize him without even thinking about it. I saw him—Andrea, his soul—without stopping to question my immediate, instinctual response to him when I left the side chapel and saw him near the altar.

And that time we accidentally bumped into each other in the rain? It was crazy and amazing.

"I don't care what you look like now. You're still you, and I still love you."

His smile broadened, his eyes—already puffy from all that crying—sparkling in pure happiness. We were ridiculous, I thought, when he leaned close for a long kiss.

Centuries-old boyfriends still acting like lovesick puppies around each other, but we were blessed enough to be allowed a second chance. I didn't know if past lives and reincarnation theories and philosophies had anything to say about our shared experiences, but it didn't matter. Papà loved me enough to give me this, and I owed it to him to live for myself and be happy with who I am.

The next few days were spent with each other, and this time I visited Luke's home and was introduced to his family. His parents were, shockingly, atheists and worked in STEM, his older twin sisters studying medicine. Luke was the dreamer of the family, which didn't surprise me at all, and he never had trouble with them when he came out. At least nobody batted an eye when I told them my current educational limbo. Luke's mom even encouraged me to continue the English Lit and Art History thing.

"Even if you don't find a job in those fields, they at least give you a solid foundation for work in the arts and humanities. Now—how about some pizza?" she said.

And for the first time in three hundred years, Luke and I made love in my room. It was a painfully exquisite moment of reacquainting ourselves with each other's bodies even if our modern selves weren't exact replicas. Everything we knew about each other went far deeper than physical selves, and I suppose romance writers would describe it more along the lines of two old souls coming together again.

There was truth in it, and if a person's heart could break from the pressure of absolute joy just as much as it did with grief, mine would have torn itself into pieces.

We lay facing each other while the rain battered the windows, spent and sweaty and smelling like come, and we found we didn't need to talk much. We just lay on our sides, facing each other, sometimes gently tracing beloved features with a finger, sometimes playing with the other's hair. And memories from three hundred years ago would surface—summer in Venice, springtime in my little town near Padua (or Padova as I called it then), my childhood and teen years.

Everything from beauty to tragedy and whatever came in between surfaced, obliged me to acknowledge them as an intrinsic part of what made me, me. Then and now, all coming together in a richly textured tapestry that would forever be unique to me and Luke, whatever the future might hold for us.

So many things happened between my final meeting with Papà and my parents' return from their retreat that I barely was able to keep track of the days. It felt like a dam had been breached, finally, and an unstoppable surge of water followed.

I continued to work, but with Luke back in my life, my mood at the warehouse soared, and I didn't even feel crushed whenever I saw Christian and Elliot together, lost to the world, talking as though they were the only people left alive. I gave them their space and even offered advice when Elliot started worrying about Christian's birthday gift.

My playlist expanded some more, much to Santiago's delight when I showed him what I was listening to. Scarlatti, Couperin, Lully, Albinoni, Corelli, and even more choral music eased my way through each day until the weekend my parents returned.

I cleaned the house top to bottom and prepared their lunch. The freak weather system was already easing with reports of flooding, destruction of houses on precarious cliffs, mudslides and avalanches wrecking coastline roads and even collapsing sections of them coming from all over. We were lucky we only had occasional power outages and some blocked storm drains, but the city got away with minor damages compared to other places.

I ran out to get some coffee since we were out, and they were back home by the time I returned.

"I thought you won't be home till this afternoon," I said, panting a little as I unpacked the bag. "I got more coffee since I kind of used it all up while you were away."

I rattled on and on about work while keeping busy, my parents having put their bags away in their bedroom and now joining me in the dining room for something to eat. I didn't even have lunch prepared yet and needed to get going on that. I also didn't realize how silent and tense the atmosphere was until I actually turned around to find them both standing near the table and watching me with grim faces.

I blinked and waited, but neither spoke. "What's wrong?" I asked.

Mom pulled something from her pocket and tossed it on the table, and I saw a couple of torn condom wrappers. I'd thrown them into my bedroom's wastebasket, which wasn't full enough for me to clear out, so I never even gave it any thought. My blood drained away from me, and a chill descended as I stared at the wrappers.

"You've been bringing men into my house?" Mom asked in that low, quiet, and dangerous tone she always used when she was controlling her anger.

I couldn't answer right away because my mind was scrambling to piece together what they were likely thinking, and those anxious phone calls of theirs with all that bizarre and offensive stuff they learned from their "friends" screamed danger. I didn't want to lie, but would it matter in the end? I knew their real views of me and my homosexuality when I came out. They barely kept things hidden and let slip too many expressions of disgust or disappointment, usually couched in words of appeasement and compromise.

They thought this was a phase, that this would be prayed away. That the right girl, once she showed up in my life, would change things for the better. I couldn't even make Dad support my academic choices, which were really nothing compared to my sexual orientation. I could easily switch fields of study. Who I am, though? No.

"I knew this was going to happen," Mom continued. "I knew it was a mistake to leave you alone for a month—to trust you with our house and our family name. Nothing good ever comes from being gay, Adam. Nothing. You don't know what our friends have said about their mistakes and all the wrong choices they made for the sake of, what, sex?"

Dad said nothing all this time and just let Mom hiss at me. They were one unit—always had been, always would be, and there was nothing left for me to do but to risk everything.

For me. For Luke. For Papà, who'd practically mortgaged his own soul for my happiness and whose unyielding love still burned in my chest and urged me to stand tall.

"Just one," I said evenly. "Just one. His name's Luke, he's my boyfriend, and I'm sorry I disappoint and disgust you both with who I am and whom I love, but there's nothing you can do about it."

"Boyfriend?" Mom echoed, her face unreadable though her eyes flashed. "Since when? You just met this boy, and you're now having sex with him?"

They always made things about me sound so tawdry and cheap, but I kept thinking about Papà and drew myself up, mentally stepping to the edge of the cliff and looking out. I had wings of wax, but I could do this.

"Mom, Dad, his name's Luke. And we've known each other forever," I replied.

The cliff fell away from under me, and my wings spread as I aimed for the sun—the bright, beautiful, life-giving sun that called to me again and again. It might have taken me three hundred years, but I finally answered.

Epilogue: Primavera

Luke and I are celebrating our sixth anniversary with a box of dark chocolates from our favorite chocolatier. This is one of the rare indulgences we enjoy since we try to stay independent and avoid help from Luke's well-meaning family, and that means a lot of economy on our part. Our apartment's nothing more than a box decorated with scattered odds and ends we fondly call our furniture, but it's clean, and we love it. We live in an old converted warehouse that's flanked by other dingy warehouses. Most of them remain unused, while the others continue wheezing through another gray day as trucks loaded with packaged food drive off and fan out in every direction.

Our living situation, I must admit, has a bohemian charm of its own. The warehouse's second life, its middle finger held up against gentrification, its confidence in the midst of urban grime. Our home reflects our dreams to some extent, the greatest of which takes more solid form on our anniversary. That's when we indulge and pretend to be somewhere else. With a little help from a dark chocolate truffle or two, we're transported, and the world is ours entirely.

It's late November now, and it's twilight. The remaining light of the day barely filters through the large, stained windows that line our walls, the absence of curtains allowing us a freer view of the bay from our second floor apartment. It's cold as usual, both outside and inside, with our heater broken. Our second-hand bed with its discolored mattress, though, takes us wherever our imagination demands.

It's spring in 18th century Venice. Luke's growing impatient with me, but I bide my time all the same. I keep him at bay with the right touches at the right places, applying the right pressure to ensure heightened pleasure without tipping him over the edge. I kiss him lightly here and there while holding a half-bitten truffle against his lips, smearing that Cupid's bow with dark sweetness till he's forced to take another bite or to flick his tongue against the melting confection and earn himself more appreciative kisses.

It's a constant battle between the two of us, with me enjoying the upperhand, mainly because I've more control, and Luke's only too happy to allow me that. In our fantasy, I'm Couperin's devotee and Luke's music master as well as his master—loosely speaking—in bed. With some imaginative enhancement, we get to pick up where we left off all those centuries ago. What if this happened instead of that? What if we'd run away as he'd wanted? What if...?

So we imagine, and history vanishes as centuries compress into this moment.

Luke has yet to learn the rudiments of efficiency. He runs on twenty-three years of crude life and awkward, ill-tempered energy. He was also born into money—a spoiled flâneur who thinks of little else but the endless pursuit of pleasure. He expects his needs to be met, and they are. I see to that—but on my terms, of course.

In our imagined world (an alternate version of the past we love pretending to), he certainly never expected to lose his virginity in the middle of practicing the maestro's *pièces de clavecin*. The situation couldn't be helped. I'd watched him struggle with the music because, in truth, he lacked the skill, and his petulance impressed and excited me.

I hold a truffle against his smeared lips, and he takes it in, chewing slowly, encouraging me to press my sticky fingers between them till he suckles, licking them clean and earning himself a reflexive grinding of my hips against his in answer. Our erections rub our stomachs, each other, spreading precum where they touch. A quiet moan escapes him.

Luke now smells of damp skin and chocolate. Sweat coats his forehead and pastes his hair against his skin in fine, pale clumps. Though I've managed to lick traces of truffles off his face and neck, I could still see faint marks where I sampled the unique and exciting taste of dark chocolate and skin heated by arousal. It's a heady mixture, and I want more.

I soothe him with a deep, lazy kiss, parting his lips further and sweeping my tongue over his teeth and smile against his mouth. I've found a god, a man, a boy, a mate, a second half, I remind myself. His arms snake around my neck to pull me down as his thighs press against my flanks, and his legs wrap around my hips. At the moment, I wonder what goes through his mind, how he imagines our fantasy unfolding before him, and I hope that I'm playing my part to perfection.

Images swim before my eyes in vague shapes and colors half-covered in shadows. The light from the wall sconces retains its muted glow, and everything seems bathed in gold. I take another piece of chocolate from the box, momentarily breaking the fantasy, and continue the opulent feeding as I hold it before

Luke and watch him thrust out his tongue for a sampling, flicking it slowly over the dark ganache piece. It begins to melt between my fingers.

We share the piece of chocolate, and he cleans my fingers between his lips as before. I pull away if only to situate myself more comfortably between his thighs. He pulls his legs up and rests them over my shoulders, readying himself while I oil my erection quickly before pushing in without so much as a word exchanged between us. He takes me in with little resistance, having done this so many times in the past. He simply lets out a brief, hissing breath through clenched teeth, storm-darkened eyes taking on a luminescence that steals my breath.

Innocence has long abandoned him. His passion for music has shifted in its direction. His music lessons have turned into long, voluptuous exercises in control, the harpsichord bearing silent and patient witness to our sticky fumblings at the keyboard.

Luke now takes me in with unmistakable assurance, slightly edged with arrogance, an arch smile curling his mouth as though he were chiding me for taking my damned sweet time with him. I can sense his blood flow around my prick, pulsing and warm and alive. When I kiss him again, I taste our indulgence, our shared fantasy, our shared dreams. I taste truffles, ganache, caramel, and cherry cordials. I feel them melting in my tongue, little by little, till I taste nothing but Luke—his youth, his excitement, his decadence. I taste Luke of eighteenth-century Venice and Luke of twenty-first century California. Apart, they tantalize me with possibilities both real and imagined. Together, they spoil me with something this side of perfection.

There's a full-length mirror standing against the nearest wall. It's old and thickly coated with dirt and grime in several places, but there's enough of the glass that remains untouched for me to catch a good enough glimpse of what's reflected in it.

I see the bed and its thick, tangled covers. Scattered on the floor are pieces of our clothing, freely mixing with each other—ivory silk and lace and sapphire velvet, buckled shoes, gloves, wigs, a gentleman's sword. And there's Luke, aroused and helplessly immobile under a force that makes itself known in the mirror as nothing more than a dim outline under patches of dirt and dust and the muted light from outside.

There's something supernaturally erotic in what I see. Luke, his legs raised and bent as though resting on something, his body moving rhythmically against the bed, his arms reaching out for a faint shadow, his lips straining to press kisses against another body that's only vaguely seen. Excitement swells even more at the sight of Luke getting fucked by something that barely exists in the mirror's world.

I fumble around for one more piece of chocolate, my cravings deepening as he reaches between us to take his erection in his hand while he watches me. I hold the piece between my lips and bend down to share another treat with Luke, who attempts to bite off a small portion but with little success. My thrusts are growing wilder, and we make a mess of things between us.

The sounds of our fucking, our bed creaking under our efforts, our voices dissolving into incoherence—they work through the patterns created by taste and smell, sight and touch. I'm drowning in sensual exuberance, my chocolate-covered mouth firmly pressed against Luke's, melted sweetness fusing our tongues as we taste each other. I pound his ass more and more furiously as though I were bent on breaking him apart.

Luke's breathing grows shallower and more rapid, and he finally tenses and releases in a series of helpless gasps that are drowned in my throat. His body's grip on my cock tightens as he spasms under me, and hot spunk marks his stomach and chest. I smell his release, the scent now adding to the primitive mixture that's taken a hold of my senses. My frayed control collapses.

With a cry, I empty myself in Luke, my body shuddering. Sweat trickles down my face and drops on him. Even perspiration becomes an extension of my body, and I can imagine it working like my hands, stroking Luke, caressing him, reassuring him in spite of economics and in spite of all that's been thrown in our way to impede our progress. Our scents, our tastes, our bodies' heat seem to have blended themselves nicely, and I can feel the mixture just as I sag against him, utterly spent.

Maybe it's an effect of our fantasy. Maybe it's the chocolate. Maybe it's all those hours leading up to the present. Whatever the reason, we're still enjoying our escape, and we're still in Venice in the spring, a city we'd loved and still do, still pretending to be people whose lives had tangled themselves so inextricably that they'd crept forward to this century like deep, relentless roots. And, oddly enough, I feel old and young and more alive than ever.

I pull out and roll over to my back, opening my eyes to an imagined vision. Our ceiling's filled with a painted idyll, decorated with scenes of love in rich meadows and among pagan gods. My sight darkens and clears itself, yet I feel a difference. I can see through shadows now. I can easily make out vague shapes in the night without straining too much. Sounds have softened. Textures have lessened their sting. The initial sensory intensity has lost its edge. And just as the fantasy fades, I try to picture a spoiled young man and his music teacher lost in a challenging lesson and lost to the world of eighteenth century Venice, the harpsichord tinkling under their efforts.

I turn and watch Luke lying beside me. His face is relaxed and calm, a peaceful visage of dreams though I know he's only resting, not asleep. His lips, still smeared with chocolate, are slightly parted, his cheeks a touch flushed with that rosy hue that now fades. I raise myself and move closer to press my lips against his. We've just marked each other with more of our chocolate indulgence, but I'm not about to clean the mess up. At least not yet. I pull away just as Luke opens his eyes and searches for me in the murkiness of our box-like apartment. I think I sense a hint of confusion, maybe panic, in his return to reality and the shadows that edge it.

In the present, there's no wealth, no idle independence, no opportunities for forced lessons in music. Couperin's devotee is gone, and so is his indolent pupil. In their place lie two young men in their twenties, their bills stacked up on the kitchen counter, their check book boasting a good amount. They've turned their backs on a painful history filled with rejection and are keeping their gaze on the horizon. The chill in their apartment reminds them of their broken heater, and their wet, tangled bodies remind them of the day's significance.

It's our anniversary, isn't it? Of course. Another autumn evening cloaks the scene outside. Calm is rarely assured till near midnight or after the usual police sirens fade into the distance.

So I kiss Luke again, pick up another piece of chocolate, and whisper random phrases in fluid Italian in his ear. Some I recall from my study of Petrarch back, way back in the day all those centuries ago, once upon a time. For Luke's sake (maybe even mine), I make one final lunge at the fantasy that's now dissolving between my fingers.

Beneath our bedroom window, the Grand Canal, crowned with a thousand points of light, creeps sluggishly through inky blackness and architectural decay. Rich and steeped in culture and history. Old, lethargic, voluptuous, and bloated with the city's putrid secrets. *Benedetto sia 'l giorno, et 'l mese, et l'anno, et la stagione, e 'l tempo, et l'ora, e 'l punto...*

Don't miss out!

Visit the website below and you can sign up to receive emails whenever Hayden Thorne publishes a new book. There's no charge and no obligation.

https://books2read.com/r/B-A-LFQC-GNBEC

BOOKS 2 READ

Connecting independent readers to independent writers.

About the Author

I've lived most of my life in the San Francisco Bay Area though I wasn't born there (or, indeed, the USA). I'm married with no kids and three cats.

I started off as a writer of gay young adult fiction, specializing in contemporary fantasy, historical fantasy, and historical genres. My books ranged from a superhero fantasy series to reworked and original folktales to Victorian ghost fiction.

I've since expanded to gay New Adult fiction, which reflects similar themes as my YA books and varies considerably in terms of romantic and sexual content.

While I've published with a small press in the past, I now self-publish my books. Please visit my site for exclusive sales and publishing updates.

Read more at https://haydenthorne.com.